LITTLE MYSTERIES

Praise For Sara Gran's Previous Mysteries

"Terrific...I love this book."
–Sue Grafton, *A is for Alibi*

"Sara Gran is a master at anything she does."
–*Crimereads*

"As if David Lynch directed
a Raymond Chandler novel." –CNN

"A completely original hybrid of mystery,
thriller, contemporary noir, dark comedy and
postmodern meditation about what it means
to be a detective." –*The New York Times*

"Sara Gran writes with scalpel-like clarity."
–George Pelecanos, *Hard Rain Falling*

"If Huraki Murakami wrote *The Wire*, it
would come out something like Sara Gran."
–Lauren Beukes, *The Shining Girls*

"...deeply intelligent fiction that cuts deep."
–Attica Locke, *Bluebird, Bluebird*

LITTLE MYSTERIES

NINE MINIATURE PUZZLES TO CONFUSE, ENTHRALL, AND DELIGHT

SARA GRAN

DREAMLAND BOOKS
LOS ANGELES

"You who read me with passion now must forever be my friends."

—Dorothy Iannone

For my readers.

CONTENTS

MAKE YOUR OWN TOOL OF PSYCHOSPIRITUAL DIVINATION

--- GUARANTEED ACCURATE - NEVER FAILS ----

Trim where indicated. Place print side down. Fold in corners where indicated. Flip, and fold inward again.

Solve Your Mystery!

Select numbers/emotional states. Repeat three times. Unfold for answer. The truth is now revealed.

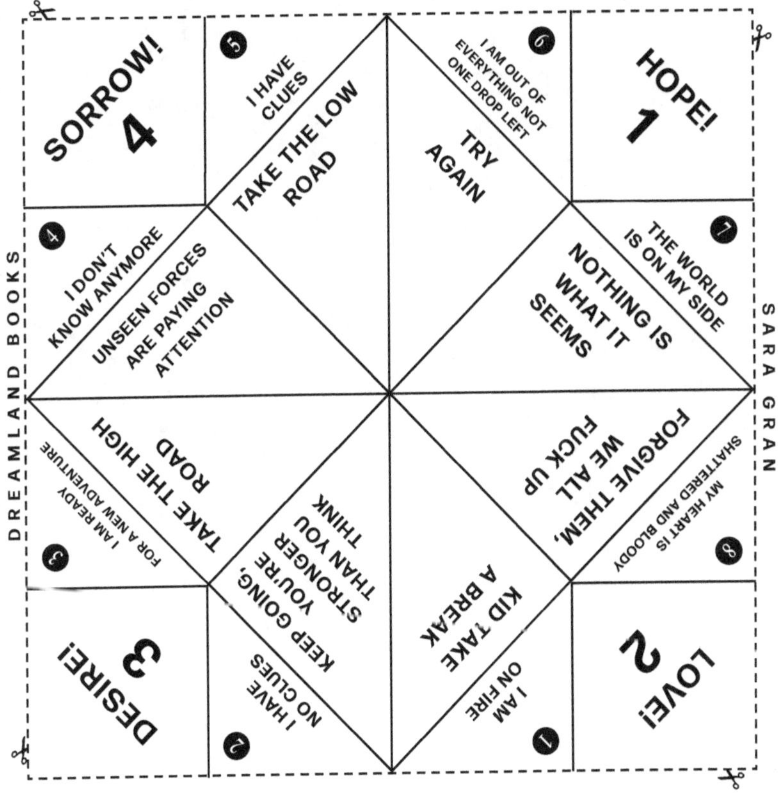

GOOD FOR: THE QUESTIONING; THE PERPLEXED; THE CURIOUS; THOSE IN TORMENT AND IGNORANCE

FIVE-MINUTE MYSTERY: THE CASE OF THE MYSTERIOUS DR. CROWLEY OR FUCK THIS WORLD INDEED!

Sheriff Brown surveyed the crime scene through sleepy and bloodshot eyes: Professor Wolf's books, papers, and household goods had been thrown around his formerly neat cottage seemingly at random, much of his exceptional china now broken, antiquarian books from his carefully curated library torn at the spine.

Old Professor Wolf explained to Sheriff Brown that he'd come home from his dawn *Naturspaziergang* to find his home in shambles. Wolf swore up and down that Dr. Crowley, a professional rival, was the one who had broken into his home, torn through everything he owned, and stolen his secret blueprints for the new space station. If Professor Wolf was to be believed, Dr. Crowley had even ripped up Professor Wolf's tomato plants in the garden, searching for his classified plans!

But while Sheriff Brown could see the state of Professor Wolf's house, he couldn't find any clues as to who had broken in, or why. Sheriff Brown, as always in the mornings, was not at his best, and struggled to fight off a hangover. Alcoholism makes detecting hard! So Cynthia Silverton, the best teen detective in the world, was called to the case.

Cynthia pulled up in her canary-yellow Cadillac, matching yellow-framed sunglasses on her face, in a charming white sundress and white kitten heels. In her yellow handbag was a Saturday night special, a deck of tarot cards, and a cyanide pill for worst-case scenarios. But today, she wouldn't need any of them.

"Hey, Cynthia," Sheriff Brown said, bleary-eyed, full of self-loathing and gin in equal measure.

Cynthia rolled her eyes. Alcoholics would always break your heart!

"Cynthia Silverton!" Professor Wolf exclaimed. "You look the spitting image of your mother. No one here seems to believe me. A very dangerous man named Dr.

Crowley has broken into my home and stolen the blue-prints to the space station we're building. I demand that Sheriff Brown arrest him immediately! And I seem to be missing some very valuable gold coins from my safe—Crowley must have taken them while he was here."

Cynthia spent exactly one minute evaluating the scene before she solved the case. But instead of telling Sheriff Brown the solution, she called Professor Wolf's estranged daughter, Elaine, on the telephone, and had a long and mysterious talk with her in the kitchen.

After her talk, Cynthia turned back to Sheriff Brown, whose hands were starting to shake as the morning wore on without a drink.

"We don't need a detective," Cynthia said to the confused and dehydrated sheriff. "There's no crime here. You can go home and sleep it off now."

What was the solution?

SOLUTION

Cynthia knew every PhD in the Rapid Falls tri-state area, and she knew there was no Dr. Crowley. She did, however, remember a villainous Dr. Crowley from one of the old detective movies she used to watch on TV as a child. And she knew that the last time Professor Wolf designed an important space station was thirty years in the past, during his heyday at the Rapid Falls Community College Department of Reverse Engineering. In a fit of confusion and terror, he had ripped up his own tomato plants, looking for gold coins he'd buried twenty years past, believing a societal collapse was near.

"You need to come and see your father," Cynthia said to Professor Wolf's daughter, Elaine, on the phone. "He has dementia. He's dying."

"Fuck this world," Elaine cried. "I guess death really does come for everyone!"

"I know," Cynthia said. "All things must die, and no amount of love can save them. It's impossible. Fuck this world indeed!"

THE MYSTERY OF THE MYCELIAL NET THAT WILL SOMETIMES, SOMEHOW, IF WE'RE LUCKY, CATCH US WHEN WE FALL

I started working for Claire DeWitt, the best detective in the world, when I was in graduate school. I'll never know if it was the best thing that ever happened to me, or the worst. Maybe it was the most interesting, and interesting is always a mixed bag.

It all started with the book, of course. When I met Claire, I was getting my PhD in medieval history. My life had been a straight, orderly, uphill expedition, accumulating degrees, publications—and, definingly, a narcissistic kind of self-esteem, propped up by approval and the mistaken idea that I was both owed this orderly life and owed it to the world. I was certain I deserved everything I had—and looking back, I think I did, although not in the way I believed at the time. I deserved a small life because I was a small person, and growing smaller by the year.

And then it all turned to sand. I was in the library at Stanford one day when a little paperback copy of *Détection* fell off a shelf and landed at my feet, like a gift. When I opened the book and read a line seemingly (seemingly!) at random—"Above all, the inner knowing of the detective trumps every piece of evidence, every clue, every rational assumption. If we do not put it first and foremost, always, there is no point in carrying on, in detection or in life."—it felt like I'd spent my life trying to fit the wrong key in a lock, and now here was the feeling of a key that fit perfectly, each tumbler falling with a satisfying little *clunk*. The more I read the book, the more I had that feeling: locks unlocking; doors opening; millions of little pieces falling into place, perfectly and slowly, an ethereal, occult Rube Goldberg machine.

Détection was a book about solving mysteries. But the more one read it, the more one realized everything was a mystery, and nothing was ever really solved, because most people prefer obfuscation to clarity, and favor soothing, slick lies over truth—including, at times, or maybe most of the time, myself. That seemed to sum up just about everything in my life so far, and the more I read it, the more something inside me seemed to crack open, and then crack further, until that which had previously been contained and orderly and content was now broken and spilled and spoiled—both within me, and in the larger, not-me world.

After spending some time with the book, I left school for a while. I went looking for Jacques Silette, the book's author, and was disturbed to find that he was long dead, with no other publications and no great analyses of his work—no Silettian study groups or research circles revealed themselves. Lost, I kept looking until I found his intellectual heirs, and *their* heirs, which led me to the controversial, although to my mind misunderstood, detective Claire DeWitt, who'd somehow ended up in a loft in San Francisco's Chinatown. We spoke for a long day in her loft and at the end of the day she hired me as her assistant, which I'd been ever since. That was nearly ten years ago. I couldn't say I exactly liked Claire back then, not right off the bat, but there was an understanding between us and the text that seemed to reframe the world and my place in it, which I soon saw had been desperately needed.

After spending some time with Claire, I went back to

school. I wasn't entirely sure why: I didn't want to teach full-time, and while I published here and there, I didn't have some big book inside me trying to wrench its way free. I had lots of ideas, but no strong desire to make an intellectual spectacle out of myself, which is what it would take to be a success in the field. The job market was abysmal in any case. But I loved the work, and I loved being in school, and I'd been in academics all of my life. It felt like home.

I can't say I solved any cases as Claire's assistant. I can say I assisted in solving forty-six. Some were small, like the Clue of the Misplaced Fortune. That was just Claire misplacing some valuable gold jewelry a client had given her to pay a bill. We found it in the bathroom of a gambling club in San Mateo. And some were big, like the Case of the Broken Sparrow, where five people died, and neither Claire nor I could sleep for days afterward. I almost gave up after that case. But we took a few weeks off, and then Claire took me up to Bodega Bay for the day and bought me oysters and chowder, my favorite meal, and went on a long walk in the bird preserve with me, and I knew that, somehow, I'd found another kind of home with her, and with this work. Claire's utter instability and unreliability reminded me of my natal home. My parents were both brilliant, volatile, charming narcissists. But, as with Claire,

I loved them anyway. If you put them all together on any given day, I could cobble together one fully functional family. Included in this lacework family was my cousin Elizabeth, my uncle Jerome, and my godmother, Helena.

And it was Helena who became my first client.

When Helena first came to me, I brought the case to Claire.

"How many cases have you worked on?" Claire asked. She was lying on her sofa watching Paul Stamets videos on her laptop.

"Forty-six," I said.

"It's time for you to solve your own case," Claire said. "You've worked for me for a few years? At least?"

"Eight and a half," I said.

"You're thirty-something?" she said.

"Yes," I said. "Exactly that."

"OK," she said. "You're ready."

I was sitting across from her. She wasn't looking at me, eyes on Paul Stamets, crouched above a turkey tail. I wasn't sure if this was Claire at her best, dazzling me with her insight into my ripeness for new responsibilities, or Claire at her worst, trying to get me to shut up and leave her to her mushrooms.

Claire paused her video, put the lid on her laptop down, and looked at me.

"Claude," she said. "This is not an impulse decision. You're ready. You know this woman. You know this world. This is your case. Go solve it. Keep the money."

I nodded. I wouldn't dream of asking Helena for money, of course, but the offer was appreciated. I still didn't stand up.

"You're still my assistant," Claire said. "I need you. You're not going anywhere. Not yet. You're just also doing this. And if it goes well, you'll do it again. Go solve your case."

Now I stood up, and I went to go solve my case.

♠

Helena was my mother's best friend from college. She looked like a lawyer: She wore conservative suits and silk blouses with unusual necklines and mid-heeled pumps. But she wasn't a lawyer; she was a professor of international literature at Stanford and a very kind woman. I didn't think she approved of my work as a detective— my parents certainly didn't—so when she texted me about lunch, I didn't anticipate she would have a case for me. I didn't anticipate anything in particular at all; we had lunch or dinner a few times a year, and if my parents weren't around, she always invited me over for the holidays.

We met at Chez Panisse and immediately I could

tell Helena was anxious. Her breath was shallow; when she tried to smile, it came out crooked and wrong.

"Helena," I said after we ordered. "I'm a detective now. And I can tell something's going on."

She looked at me for a long time, with a look on her face as if she was about to get a painful injection.

"I feel—" she said. She stopped and started again. "I'm very proud of you, Claude. You're an adult now. And I know you can help me, and I'm going to ask for your help. But I also feel…I feel like I'm falling, and I don't know if the world will catch me. I screwed up. I screwed up very, very badly." She took a deep breath. "I feel *old*," she said. She scrunched up her face and tried not to cry. "I think I'm going to lose Henry. I think I'm going to lose everything."

"Aunt Helena," I said. I used to call her that when I was a kid. "I don't know about the world. But *I've* got you. And whatever you need, I'm here."

She took a deep breath and controlled her tears.

"So tell me," I said. "Start anywhere. Just start."

"OK," Helena said. "I'll start at the beginning."

But she didn't start. Our food came. Helena got a goat-cheese-and-pumpkin pizza. I got cranberry roast duck. As you can guess from the menu, it was just past Thanksgiving.

We tried our food and talked about how perfect it was. Of course it was perfect. It was Chez Panisse.

Finally I said, "Aunt Helena. Please. Tell me."

There was a perfection to Helena, a kind of grace in the way she carried herself, that I found alternately soothing and suspicious. Helena was an elegant Black woman who sometimes seemed to be from another era, always with the right words on the tip of her tongue and peppermint candy in her purse for other people's children. But there was also a rigidity to her. She never dressed down. There wasn't much room for flaws, and I'd come to learn that flaws had substantial possibilities, and even merit. Flaws were what created life. A sperm and an egg bumped into each other and fused. A rotted cabbage became sauerkraut.

"I made a mistake," Helena said, looking down at her pizza. "A mistake with Henry. Please, have some," she said. "It's too much."

I knew she meant the pizza. But I thought maybe she also meant her guilt. She'd been married to Henry for about twenty years. He was a good person; he ran an aid group for academic refugees.

"Mistake?" I said.

Helena kept her eyes on her pizza. "Take a piece," she said. "Please. It's just too big for me to handle."

I took a piece of her pizza. Helena looked at me. "There was a woman. At Stanford. A math professor. We had—ugh, there's no good word for it. I can't believe I did it. We had an *affair*. Not a real affair. One evening and two afternoons. Once at a hotel and then twice at my house. Henry was at work. I never…we were friends, good friends, and we just. I don't know. I just felt so. I don't know. I don't understand it. I have, otherwise, been a very faithful wife. You know that."

"I do," I said. "So you had an…indiscretion. A mistake. Is she going to tell Henry?"

"No, never," Helena said. "She wouldn't do that. It's this."

Helena took a nine-by-twelve manila envelope out of her purse and gave it to me. I opened the envelope. There was a letter inside, printed on an ink-jet printer. Drugstore paper. Nothing traceable. I tried to hold it by the very edge as I read:

I KNOW WHAT YOU DID

I looked at Helena.

"There were three," she said. "Or four. I threw them out at first. I didn't know what to make of them. I didn't know they would keep coming."

Tears fell from Helena's eyes.

"Claude," she said. "I'm terrified. You don't know what it's like to get older. I can't start again. I don't want to lose everything."

Helena was, maybe, fifty-five—certainly not old. But she and Henry had built their lives as an intertwined network of friends and work and family. If she lost Henry, she wouldn't just lose her husband, awful as that would be. She would lose the life they'd carefully composed for all these years. It was a life that seemed confining to me—exactly the life I was scared of ending up in—but it was hers, and it was what she wanted, and she was my godmother, my friend, and now, my client.

"Don't worry," I said. "Your godson is a professional detective, and I'm going to solve this for you."

She tried to look relieved, but she couldn't quite pull it off. I wanted her to trust me more. But she would.

We talked about her life a bit more, looking for any obvious leads. None arose. Helena and Henry lived in verdant, prosperous Palo Alto, near the university. They were having a little party at their house on Sunday for a colleague who'd won the Thimbleton Award, which was a big deal in the world of international translations. Helena and Henry were part of a community of international academics and writers and nonprofit people who lived in and around Berkeley and Stanford.

This was my first time turning my detective eyes, as Claire called them, on my own world, and the effects weren't entirely pleasant. Helena had always been a bit of a mother figure for me, my own mother being somewhat distant and entirely nuts, if occasionally sweet. Now, for the first time, I looked at Helena as an ordinary woman, and it reduced her. The magical, maternal qualities I'd assigned her were slipping away. She'd made bad choices, and felt shame over them. An aging human in a weakening body who wanted excitement and security in equal measures. One of the first things you learn as a detective is that this is a fundamental human paradox: Excitement versus security. Known versus unknown. Pleasure versus safety. All variations on a theme.

As a boy, I would have imagined Helena free from such quotidian problems. Now, as a man, after an initial adjustment, they made me appreciate her all the more.

At the end of lunch, out on Shattuck Avenue, I gave her a big hug. I was nearly a foot taller than her.

She looked at me, a question on her face, one she needed answered.

"Helena," I said. "People make mistakes. Forgive yourself."

She still looked at me, the question stronger now.

"There's not a thing on this earth that could make me think less of you," I said. I chose my next words very carefully. "The life you've had—I appreciate the level of perfection you've achieved. Your enormous accomplishments. But perfection, for me, is not a goal in and of itself. Life is here to live. And living is messier than I think either of us would like."

Helena finally hugged me back.

"Thank you," she said.

"I love you," I said. "We're going to fix this."

I knew she was trying to believe me.

♠

On Sunday I went to Helena and Henry's for the Thimbleton party. Helena and Henry lived in a white cottage from the 1930s, kept so neat and clean it almost seemed frozen: trimmed hedges under the windows, some small purple flowers on long green stems that I couldn't name (Claire would be disappointed) but every suburban home in the Bay seemed to have clustered around the doors. They were related to onions, or maybe it was garlic, or both.

I parked in front of a house across the street from Helena's. It was easily a ten-million-dollar property, not more than five years old, and atrocious. Two Teslas in the driveway. I hated to admit how much I'd come to judge people, but I had, and my first thought was: *Tech people, too much money, never home.*

A little girl was standing in the yard.

"Hello," I said to the girl. She was a white girl, maybe eleven or twelve, wearing blue jeans and sneakers and a T-shirt. There was something immature about her, and not in an appealing way. She wasn't cute. She stared at Helena and Henry's house.

She glared at me.

"What's the party for?" she asked.

"For a friend of Helena and Henry's," I said. "He won a prize. Are you coming?"

"I wasn't invited," she said.

"I'm sure they'd love to have you," I said. I had no idea how to talk to children. I always spoke to them like adults, with mixed results.

Apparently I'd done it wrong this time, because the little girl turned her back to me and stood facing her house. I left her and crossed the street.

Henry and Helena's house was tasteful and comfortable and close to perfect inside—neutral colors, good furniture, always a fully stocked kitchen, bar, and guest room, where I'd stayed many times. The party was uneventful and pleasant. About twenty people. I thought maybe I was getting a cold, until I remembered that this was what boredom felt like. There was nothing for me to see here. I asked some subtle questions and got nowhere. If anyone here had it out for Helena, they had an excellent poker face. I made an excuse—a paper to finish—and left.

Henry walked me to my car. Henry was from Spain and spoke six languages and had been in seminary to be a priest before he left to start his nonprofit. People kept throwing grant money and NGO contracts at him. He gave money away as fast as he could, but it still kept finding him.

"You need anything?" he said as we walked to my car. He always asked that. He was offering me money without being crude. I felt, in that moment, like I needed everything: intelligence, insight, courage. But no one could give you those things—it seemed like a kind of cruel joke in life that one had to generate everything that allowed one to generate anything.

"I don't," I said. "Thanks, though."

"So how's this detective business?" Henry asked. He lit a cigarette. Bad European habits. I didn't think he'd mind so much if he found out about Helena and her friend. I thought he would understand that a momentary indulgence didn't mean Helena loved him any less. But she didn't want him to know, and she was my client.

"It's good," I said. "I like it. I think I'm sticking with it."

Henry put a hand on my back. "Good," he said. "Good, kid. Good for you."

I was nearly forty, but he meant it with affection, and I took it that way. Henry hugged me and went back inside, after being sure to tell me again to call him if I needed anything.

♠

My next step was to meet the woman Helena had the affair with. Her name was Roslyn and she was, as Helena said, a math professor at Stanford. I showed up at her office during office hours, knocked, and in response to her confused look said, "I'm here about Helena."

She frowned and invited me in. I sat down. Roslyn was in her forties and Japanese-American. I knew from the research I'd done that she was from Minnesota and was very good at what she did—something to do with probability and philosophy. She had long shiny salt-and-pepper hair with short bangs and no makeup except red lipstick, perfectly applied to her lips. She wore a structural black dress I didn't understand.

I told her what was happening to Helena. She frowned again.

"That's terrible," she said. "I hope she knows I had

nothing to do with the letters. We had a few…encounters. She's a dear friend. I would never want to hurt her."

She was telling the truth. We talked some more but she didn't have anything useful to add. I liked Roslyn. She seemed genuinely concerned with Helena. She was emotional and there was something poetic about her.

"I miss her," Roslyn said, as I stood up to leave. "Helena. We were friends. We don't have to—we don't have to do that again if she doesn't want to. But I miss her and Henry."

"I'll tell her," I said. Spontaneously, Roslyn hugged me, and I hugged her back.

"Fix this for her," Roslyn said.

"I will," I said.

But it wasn't that easy. I spent the rest of the day poking around Stanford, asking questions, watching Helena's office, seeing who had access to her life. There were no big shocks. No big surprises. Helena had no enemies and, other than the affair with Roslyn, no big secrets.

I was glad to get back to dirty, vibrant Berkeley.

Two more weeks passed. I started to grow anxious. Helena grew much more anxious. After the Sunday party there had been another letter: YOU WERE WRONG, this one said. Wrong about what? When? I couldn't figure it out. Helena had started having panic attacks at night, she told me. When we met for dinner at Quince to go over what I'd found so far, Helena looked older. She seemed brittle, and for the first time since I'd known her, she was a little short with her words.

"You have nothing?" she said, jaw tense, shoulders set high. "How is that possible?"

"These things take time," I said, which sounded like a horrible response even as I said it. I could see what little faith she had in me draining away. Worse was the sight of something else draining away—some combination of joy and softness and attention that, I saw now, I hadn't fully appreciated in Helena until it was almost gone.

I felt terrible.

A few days later I had lunch with Claire at a Burmese restaurant in the Sunset District. Over catfish and okra I told her about the case.

"Stop trying to be a good friend," Claire said. "Or a good son. Or a good anything. I know this is your crowd, and you want them to know you're a great detective. They don't need to know that. Only you need to know that."

She was right. I was too eager for a solution, for the wrong reasons, and that wouldn't help. I couldn't beat the feeling that there was something just before my eyes that I couldn't yet see.

"Question everything," Claire reminded me. "Believe nothing. Follow the clues."

With that, I got back to work.

♠

It was nearly twenty days into the case. Of course I had fingerprinted the letters. Both, unfortunately, were a mess—no full prints, nothing I could use. No postmarks—they'd been hand-delivered. Claire and I had both done plenty of research on envelope identification and I knew right away that would be a dead end. None of this was a surprise.

It was close to three a.m. and I was sitting in my studio in Berkeley, looking at the clues I'd assembled—the letters and the envelopes. That was it. I doubted not only my ability to solve the case, but every decision I'd made that had left me here.

Maybe I couldn't do this. What if I didn't make it as a detective? What if I wasn't good enough? What if my life was just a long river of passive-aggressive tenure fights and cocktail parties and pretending not to be jealous when other people won awards? This world that I'd had such mixed feelings for all my life—what if that was it for me? What if the larger, more interesting life was for other people, not me?

I got up and paced around the room. The more I let these thoughts infect me, the more they took over until I could hardly think about the case at all. I worked myself up into a kind of state that was rare for me. I was, and am, an emotional man. But my life had always put me in positions where I had to keep those emotions tightly contained.

Now, though, there was no reason to contain myself. My emotions, untrained and feral, were threatening and hurtful. Why did I think I could be a detective? How could I have done this to Helena? She'd put her faith in me, and I was letting her down. In my wild thoughts I imagined Helena's fear would come true and Henry would find out. Helena wouldn't forgive me, and they'd shut me out of their lives forever. I saw myself parking across from their house, as I'd often done, a party inside, but now I wasn't invited in.

And then it happened.

It was something I'd heard about before, read about many times, but never actually experienced. And it was different and stronger and better than I ever thought it would be. It was the satisfaction of orgasm without the stickiness of bodily fluids or other people. It was the key fitting in the lock, and all the tumblers sliding into perfect place. It was the sun breaking through the clouds just as you got to the beach.

"Wow," I said to my empty room. "Hey. Hello. Wow."

I'd solved the case.

It was three a.m. I thought maybe I should wait till morning. Then I thought: *Claire would do it now.*

So I did it now. It was a week before Christmas. I washed and dressed and drove down to Palo Alto and parked in the same spot across the street from Helena and Henry's house, in front of the ten-million-dollar Apple-store property. The ten-million-dollar house was quiet and dark.

It was close to five. I watched Helena's house anxiously. At 5:55, a light went on.

I texted Helena. She met me outside in a pair of flannel pajamas and a plaid bathrobe with a confused look on her face.

I opened the passenger door. She got in the car.

"What is it?" she asked.

"I solved the case," I said. "I think."

Her face relaxed. After a deep breath and a long sigh she looked ten years younger.

"But," I said, "Did I ever explain to you the difference between a crime and a mystery?"

"No," Helena said, looking worried again. "I didn't know there was a difference."

"A crime is the letter you got," I said. "The crime, in

this case, being harassment. So we can find out who did that, and I think I have found out who did it, and deal with them. But then there's still the mystery. And the mystery is…"

I struggled to explain the distinction. I'd never put it into my own words before.

"The mystery is the hole that's been created in the fabric of your life," I said.

Helena looked at me. My metaphor didn't work for her. My pedagogy skills were a little embarrassing.

"The mystery," I said, repeating a line I'd heard Claire use to good effect before, "is a little patch of the world that's been bent, and we need to set it right."

Now Helena gave me a *look*. It was not flattering to either of us. I was losing her. I gave it one more try.

"The mystery," I said, "is the situation or fact or lack or feeling or patch of existence that no one wants to look at. And in that spot, where no one wanted to look, there was an opportunity for a crime."

"Oh," Helena said. "Oh."

She understood.

Just then the door to the ten-million-dollar house opened. The little girl came out through the front door. She was alone again, and she was scowling again. She had a heavy backpack on her back. There were two Teslas in the driveway and she was walking toward the bus stop to take the bus to school.

I opened the car door and got out and met the girl on the curb.

"Hey," I said.

The girl saw Helena in the car and shot her a dirty look.

"What's your name?" I said to the girl.

"What do you care?" she said.

"Because you've been making life really hard for one of my best friends," I said. "And now you're going to stop."

The girl looked panicked, and before I could anticipate it, she started to run. The sun was coming up but it was still foggy and dim. I chased after her. Neither of us was terribly athletic. I caught her around the corner. I grabbed the collar of her sweatshirt and she started to make a sound and I said, "Don't. Just don't."

She didn't. She stopped and started to cry. First she just sniffed a little. Then, more quickly than I thought possible, she was sobbing and heaving, viscous fluids dripping from her face.

"She has everything," the girl said, through her sobs. "She had everything and she didn't even want it."

I crouched down so our eyes were level. She was stiff and uncomfortable.

"What's everything?" I asked. "What did Helena have?"

"She has Henry," the girl wailed. "She has Henry and she has you and all those people who are over all the time. She has everything and she doesn't appreciate any of it. She doesn't even care. She let that other woman come over and ruin everything. She had everything and she ruined it. Now she has to pay. Some people have nothing. I bet you didn't know that, because you're stupid like she is. But some people have fucking nothing."

She'd been studying Helena's life for months, maybe years, from her yard. I felt a flood of shame of how dismissive I'd been of Helena and Henry's life of warmth and cheer and good deeds. What had seemed so dull a few weeks ago was, through the girl's eyes, a paradise of care and love. How lucky I'd been, and still was, to be a part of it.

The little girl started to sob again, odd sounds pouring out of her like an animal. I noticed no one had come looking for her.

"Fuck her," the girl said. "I hate her. I hate her so much."

Helena caught up with us, still in her pajamas.

Helena looked at the girl and looked at me.

"What on earth?" Helena said.

"Helena," I said. "Meet your criminal."

The girl ran away. Helena and I watched her run. Helena looked sad and her brow was troubled.

The crime was solved. The mystery, I wasn't sure.

♠

On Christmas Eve, Helena and Henry had their usual party. This year my father was at a symposium in Sweden and my mother was visiting family in Paris. I drove to Palo Alto as the sun was going down. Christmas with academics was always a mixed bag. They all tended to get depressed around the holidays. If not, they might try to be clever and question the politics of Christmas carols and the morality of ham. It could be a chore.

But this year, immediately, things were different. To begin with, instead of the usual tasteful white lights hanging from the porch, there was a large, tacky, bright, blow-up Santa in front of the house, in garish red and green. And there was music coming from the house, not the usual classical or jazz or mild Christmas songs, but joyful Stevie Wonder. Claire had once observed that everyone loves Stevie Wonder, and over the years I'd found she was correct.

And the biggest surprise of all: When I opened the door, along with the usual twenty or thirty guests, there was Roslyn. She was wearing a different strange black outfit, but this time her lipstick was a little crooked. And she was drunk, and smiling.

"Claude!" she said. She hugged me and laughed like we were old friends. I hugged her back.

"Come," she said. "Have a drink!" We made our way to the kitchen, where she made me an eggnog with rum.

"Thank you," Roslyn said to me, with one more hug. "Thank you for giving me my friend back."

Roslyn disappeared into the party. I followed her out to the living room. It was the same party I'd been to for at least a dozen Christmas Eves, but somehow, it felt entirely different. If their previous parties were bloodless, this one had some blood.

Across the room I saw Helena and Henry standing together, talking to the Porters, a dull couple who taught literature at Berkeley. Both Henry and Helena looked bright and happy and—although it was a bit odd to think of them that way—like they'd had sex sometime that day.

Standing between them was the girl from across the street. The tiny blackmailer. Helena and Henry each held one of her hands. A cheap red Santa hat was on the girl's head. Every few moments either Helena or Henry looked down at her or squeezed her hand or smiled at her.

The girl looked like a different child. She smiled and fidgeted and laughed like an ordinary girl.

I didn't know what had happened. But somehow, I wasn't surprised.

I couldn't stay long at the party. I had another party to go to, with some friends from school, in Oakland. Tomorrow, Christmas Day, Claire had us staking out a hot dog stand in San Rafael for the Case of the Broken Tooth.

Not a bad way to spend the holidays.

The world needed more people like Helena. People who would catch you if you fell. That night I articulated something to myself that I'd always known, but never put into words: that Helena would catch me if I needed catching. I couldn't count on my parents, and the rest of my blood relatives were scattered around the world, and not reliable. But I knew, even though we'd never said it out loud, that I had a home with Helena, wherever she was. I only realized now, in the hot, bright Christmas party, that Helena was why I had come out all right.

I made my way to Henry and Helena and the girl to say goodbye. Now Roslyn was standing with them. Roslyn hugged me again. I didn't understand the relationship among the three of them—who knew what or who was sleeping with who. But they were all happy, and they all had that look of lightness and relief that people have after a mystery is solved. A little raw and wet, like a chick just out of an egg. Born anew.

Henry asked me again if I needed anything, which made Helena and me laugh. But I appreciated it. Maybe someday I would.

I was ready to leave when the Porters spotted me, and I was stuck with them for a few minutes before I could get out. A few yards away I saw Helena take the little girl to the buffet and help her make a plate piled high with ham and potatoes and greens.

Helena leaned down and spoke into the girl's ear as they looked out at the party together.

"Look," Helena said. "Look at how lucky we are."

I looked out at the party with them. Of course these people were imperfect. All people are flawed. Flaws are where life comes from.

The girl beamed, a smile so wide her face could hardly hold it.

I left and got in my car. My phone rang before I made it to the highway. It was Claire. I knew she was calling to congratulate me on solving my first mystery. I didn't pick up. I knew that she knew why I would want to keep this moment to myself. And I knew that she knew it would mean the world to me that she'd wanted to share it with me.

I still wasn't sure if meeting Claire was the best thing that ever happened to me, or the worst. But I did know that I wouldn't have traded this moment for anything.

Someone was falling, someone I loved, and I'd caught them. I'd always felt a half-step away from other people, removed from the real life of life. Now, for the first time, I felt like I was a part of that life. I liked it. I wanted more.

I realized I'd never named the case. I'd ask Claire for help with that later. But I knew it was closed. I accelerated onto the highway and back home.

Although truthfully, at that moment, the whole world felt like home, and I knew I wanted to do this for the rest of my life.

THE END

THE GOOD SMELL OF NEW YORK CITY / THE OCEAN-SALTED AIR

1988

You are Claire DeWitt, the greatest teen detective in the world. You are standing on the corner of Rivington and Ludlow Streets on the Lower East Side of New York City. It has been a long night of nightclubs and bars and minor crimes; early in the evening, maybe, you were on a case, but you've forgotten that case now. The Case of the Silver…What was it exactly? Something about metals. You hope

2020

You are Claire DeWitt, the best detective in the world. You are standing at the junction of the Venice Boardwalk and Windward Avenue in Los Angeles. It's been a long day: walking, swimming, running. After a rough spell involving many mistakes, some bad luck, and a number of threats from doctors regarding losing a limb, you are trying to get back in fighting shape. Literally. Detectives need you wrote it down, or someone did, because facts are slipping out of your head like water out of a faucet. Water out of a faucet: An ugly image crosses your mind: a man lying on Ninth Street, a hole in his head, blood pouring out...Did that happen? It did happen. He'd been shot or who knows what. Yesterday, or the day before yesterday. Was it the case? No, just someone you happened to walk by. You ran to a payphone and called 911 but didn't approach him. Instead you watched from the corner and waited for the ambulance to come and when it didn't come you called again, got snapped at by the 911

to fight, at least your kind of detective, at least you. You can and will fight with one leg, but two is better. So every day: a swim, a walk, a run, weights as heavy as you can bear, a protein shake for breakfast and a poke bowl for lunch and a steak for dinner, trying to build back what you have given away to time and age and chance. You want it all back.

You've been asked to stay home. Everyone's been asked to stay home. No one knows yet that you don't get it outside.

You run outside anyway, in the ocean-salted air. You guess you should be lady for calling twice, exchanged words, and left.

You were scared of his blood.

♠

Stickers and posters and graffiti on the wall read: *silence=death, God made Adam and Eve not Adam and Steve, party's over,* and a long block of poster-text about laboratory origins that you can't read—the type is too small and you are too drunk and high.

The witness you met earlier that night had the

scared of the virus but you're already full to the limit with other fears: age, death, losing money, losing your leg, never having sex again.

♠

Graffiti on the boardwalk reads: *fear is the real virus, plandemic, scamdemic, be kind wear a mask, spread love not the virus.*

Running, you pass by fewer people every day, each of you shifting trajectories to avoid each other's air, often glaring and fearful. Some days you see no one else at all.

Weeks pass and you're not stronger. It's different when you're older.

virus. You know you won't get it just from being in the room with her, but it's disconcerting to be so close. It feels like it's coming closer to you, or maybe you're getting closer to it. Exposure feels imminent. She said it was pneumonia but you can tell. Everyone can tell. A junkie living on the Lower East Side her whole life, shooting dope since before people knew to use bleach, rail-thin, sores on her face. It didn't look hopeful.

Everyone just wants to live.

♠

You're closer to sober and healthy than you've ever been but muscle isn't growing. You finally get to see a doctor, everyone masked and goggled and gloved, whispering about hospitals collapsing and can you get it from groceries? It's revealed you are out of everything: hormones, vitamins, minerals, beneficial bacteria. You take IVs, pills, patches; more weeks pass and finally you're getting stronger.

♠

You're staying in a motel a few blocks from the beach. Your neighbor has the virus. He left a note on your door so you wouldn't come too close. No one

You're on the corner because you're waiting for your cocaine dealer. Carmen is maybe ten years older than you, and stronger and tougher. She's from the projects on the Lower East Side and you suspect she has rarely, in her life, had the opportunity not to be tough. Once she met you at a bar at a Mexican restaurant on Avenue A to sell you drugs and stayed for a margarita; you found out Carmen had a daughter who lived with her aunt, and was planning to go to school to become a nurse. She'd been a CNA for a while, and liked it, but the money wasn't good enough. But then, not yet as skilled a detective

knows: Can you get it through walls? Through a mask? But sometimes you can't stop thinking about him and so you go over and knock on his door and you talk through the closed door. You ask if he needs anything and he never does. He complains about trying to get a doctor or nurse on the phone. He doesn't feel too bad but his breathing keeps getting worse.

All day, every day, you hear sirens, carrying away the sick, arriving for the dead.

Then one day he asks for something: vanilla ice cream. You go out to pick up a pint of vanilla ice (or person) as you would become, you asked why her daughter didn't live with her.

"What the fuck are you asking for?" Carmen said, offended. "Mind your own fucking business. That got nothing to do with you."

Carmen walked out of the bar, angry.

This is the first time she's returned your page since, calling you at a payphone.

cream for him and you come back and paramedics are carrying him away. You've never seen his face and you don't see it now, covered by an oxygen mask, but you see he has patchy gray and blond hair and wears a UMich sweatshirt and blue pajama pants with dignified white stripes.

On a gurney, surrounded by masked paramedics, he sees you holding the paper bag of ice cream and gives you the thumbs-up.

"I'll put it in the freezer for you," you say. "Come over when you get back." He nods with exhausted enthusiasm. But he never comes back. It is, after all,

She was cold, but agreed to sell to you.

Paging her had seemed like a good idea but now you don't want it. Any of it. Now you think that ecstasy pill you took was not, in fact, ecstasy, because you are feeling very far from ecstatic. Your mind skims back over the last ten hours: There were drinks, a few lines, two pills you were promised were quaaludes (Were they? Do dreams come true? No.), more drinks, more lines, a pill you were promised was ecstasy (Was it? Can you trust the girl in the bathroom who sold it to you? Are we surrounded by angels? Also no.).

a motel, and the ice cream becomes crystalline and stiff in your freezer.

Everyone just wants to live.

♠

There is a small band of homeless people you see on your run every day, just about where the boardwalk begins at Windward. The camp is smaller every day as more of the residents accept hotel vouchers that the city is giving away. There is one woman who maybe you know from some past adventure. Something in her face is familiar. You asked her about it once.

"Do I know you?" you

You are fading, you realize. You are fading away to nothing.

♠

So: everything seems to be sliding out of your head, including any knowledge of self. And now you feel that you, yourself, are sliding down. That strange gelatinous feeling is, it turns out, your knees as they softly lose the will to keep you upright. Now it's spreading to your hips and up your spine, and everything is curling up black around the edges. You've been here before, you think; this is a thing that happens. And now you are on the pavement, smelling the good smell of New York City. Later,

asked, slipping her a wrinkled twenty.

But she said, "I don't think so," and then, seeing the bill, "Oh! Thanks!"

After that, you swing by a couple times a week with a twenty or a ten for her. You ask her name once and immediately forget it. Carmen? Maybe. Is she spending the money you give her on drugs? Probably. Would you, if you lived on the board-walk? You've OD'd in four-star hotels so: yes.

Carmen is familiar both in that you think you've specifically met before and in that she feels like home, so you're not someone will tell you that this is when the seizure began. Just when Carmen got out a taxi, ready to sell you a forty-dollar bag.

You don't remember what happened. Later, people will tell you that other people came running. Three of them ran from the corner, young professionals slumming. They ran to you and bent down and looked at you and not one of them would touch you.

The person who tells you that, a Puerto Rican man of fifty-six named Sergio who saw you fall from across the street, looks down with shame when

surprised when she tells you she's from New York City, too. She's kind and tough in equal measure, like you remember older women in the neighborhood you grew up in (you are now an older woman yourself, but one clinging to youthful strength, not having acquired enough insight or wisdom to let the past go and fill the absence with the present day). Last time you saw Carmen she was yelling at another member of her camp who'd stolen her friend's drugs: The man was bigger than her, and younger, but Carmen was righteous in defense of her friend and scared the man off.

he tells you this in the weeks to come, when you're investigating the scene of your own little crime. And you know he's ashamed because he wouldn't even cross the street.

"You know," he says. "Everyone's scared."

♠

Then, Sergio tells you, Carmen got out of her taxi. She saw you on the ground and ran over.

"She looked around," Sergio says. "She saw that no one was doing nothing. So she just makes this face and shrugs and—" Sergio shrugs to illustrate.

But then she caught you looking and yelled at you, too: "Mind your own business," she shouted. "This got nothing to do with you."

♠

Now, today, you're catching your breath after a run. The entire camp is gone and no one is on the boardwalk—or so you think, until you see Carmen across the board-walk, on the beach side. At first you think she's looking at you and you wave and then you realize she's looking at nothing and then you see that she's leaning forward, and evermore forward still. You trot over, thinking all will be forgiven and you'll

"And then she jumps in. She says, 'You're going to be OK,' and then she—"

He makes a gesture with his hand, a gesture of jumping in.

♠

Carmen gave you mouth-to-mouth while someone else called an ambulance. She was scared of cops, so she left as soon as you were breathing again. The paramedics slapped you around a little and put some oxygen on you

help her settle down on a bench.

But that doesn't happen. Instead she falls to the ground and starts shivering and then vomits up yellow bile. Then her eyes roll back in her head.

You run toward her and then you stop. You don't want to touch her.

Everyone's scared.

♠

You look at Carmen for a second, willing her to get better. She doesn't. She stops breathing, and she looks like she's going to die.

You think of all the times strangers have saved your

and brought you to the ER. You're in the medical ward for two days and then the psych ward for three more.

When they let you out you get on the F train and take it out to Coney Island and walk to the beach. The ocean is freezing cold but you take off your boots and tights and tie up your dress, soiled and foul-smelling from your adventures, and walk into the water up to your thighs. And you think: *I can be born again, over and over. But somehow I am always still myself.*

life. The risks others have taken, without which you'd be gone.

You jump in.

♠

You wipe fluids off Carmen's mouth and give her rescue breathing. Her lips are hot and dry. Your heart is racing and you know when it's over you'll be terrified, but now you're too busy to be scared.

"You're going to be OK," you say, not knowing if it's true.

Finally someone else comes wandering over looking for dope and you scream, "Narcan, now."

♠

It takes you a while to track Carmen down. She doesn't respond when you page her. You vaguely know she's from the Avenue D projects but it takes a lot to find out more, your type not being particularly welcome among the teenagers of the Riis Houses. Finally you find her apartment, thirteen days later, at the end of a dimly lit, littered hallway.

She's having a party, with red lights and pounding

He doesn't have any but he goes and finds a kit and comes back in three or thirty or three hundred minutes. He's a skinny Black man who looked young from a distance but now, closer, you see he's old, and been in this life a long time, arms covered in scars. Together you figure out how to administer it and after the second dose she comes around, confused and angry and not entirely here. She doesn't seem to recognize you at all or understand what just happened.

When the paramedics approach, you tell them everything you know and split. You go down to the cold ocean and take off music. She's not happy to see you and says nothing when she sees you at her door. Instead she looks at you, face still and hard as stone.

"I just wanted to say thank you," you say. "I think you saved my life."

"I DID save your life," she says. "Don't bother me again."

And she slams the door in your face.

You go home.

THE END

your shoes and, in T-shirt and running shorts, walk into the cold water up to your waist. And you think: *I can be born again, over and over. But somehow I am always still myself.*

♠

You get the virus and it knocks you out for thirteen days. You try to call your doctor but no one answers. Your friend Nick Chang mails you herbs that you're too sleepy and weak to make into a tea. At one point, when you get scared, you call a rich person who owes you a favor, and through the channels of wealth she finds and sends you a nurse who stays for a few hours and gives you more

IVs and tests and a few shots: vitamins, minerals, hydration. Her name is also Carmen, and she is also from New York City. She tells you you'll be OK.

When you get better, you slowly start running on the boardwalk again. All your newfound strength is lost, and you have to start again.

You look for Carmen, your Carmen, but you never see her again. A month later, one of the men from her camp tells you she recovered OK, and went back to live with her daughter in New York.

"She ain't any of your business," the man says as you

leave. "Don't bother her again."

You feel like a door has been slammed in your face.

You keep running.

THE END

THE CASE OF THE JEWEL IN THE LOTUS
OR
THE MYSTERY YOU WILL NEVER QUITE SOLVE, BUT IF YOU'RE LUCKY, WILL COME A LITTLE CLOSER TO EVERY DAY UNTIL DEATH

The problem was money. I was just about thirty. I'd been a working detective since I was twelve. I didn't need a lot of money, but I needed some, and I didn't have any. Fees from the last few jobs had gone, variably, to a guy I was sleeping with who didn't have a car and a girl I knew who was trying to keep her mother in a nursing home and a trip to Mexico City that lasted too long and cocaine. I was staying in a room-by-the-week hotel in San Francisco for what I thought would be a few months and turned into a few decades.

A lesbian PI I knew in Sacramento, Lisa Tanning, always had more work than she could handle. Her cases weren't like my cases, which tended to drag on for months or sometimes years. I was already developing a reputation as the detective of last resort. Lisa's cases were easier and faster and would make money now. In the past she'd tried to interest me in her overflow, which I always declined. Now I called her up and told her I needed fast money and she had a case for me within a day.

Lisa was OK. More than OK. She was a good egg, if there were any good eggs left. She came from Sacramento high society, or the facsimile thereof. Pretty much her whole trade was dealing with people's little personal messes and fuck-ups. No murders, no big crimes. Fine by me.

I solved the case for Lisa. It was too boring to talk about. A man, an affair, money embezzled, all of it dull. I got ten grand for one week—detecting fee plus finder's fee. Next was another boring case: a mother, a daughter, a freshly-dead grandmother, some stolen jewelry that was easily recovered in a safe deposit box, family secrets brought to light and unforgiven, eight grand for me.

The next case was supposed to be just as easy and equally forgettable. It was a divorce case. The wife had an undiagnosed, vague, system-wide ailment that no doctor could pinpoint but prevented her from doing anything practical. She was yanking at everyone's heartstrings to get more out of the divorce because of it. The husband's mother hired us to prove the wife was faking. An easy ten grand for a week or two of work.

Or so it seemed. The case is not the mystery, and the mystery is not the crime—and if you're looking for logic, look elsewhere, and good luck, because I have yet to see any in this life.

The mother was part of Lisa's circle. She was in her sixties and her face was as tight as a bedsheet, not from surgery, but from rage. The money, at least some of it, was *her* money, emotionally if not legally, money her father had made in something idiotic and luck-stricken and passed down to her. No way was this sick-every-day whining-all-the-time not-working wife getting an extra red cent.

The next week I watched the wife. She lived in a luxe Craftsman in the nice part of Sacramento, not far from Lisa. Her name was April. As predicted, she didn't really go anywhere. She left the house every two days or so to go to one alternative practitioner or another—homeopath, acupuncturist, hypnotist. She spent the rest of her time at home, alone.

When she was home I sat in a car across the street from her house. April's curtains were down but she'd hung them an inch away from the glass, so if you positioned yourself right you could see bits and pieces of what went on inside around the margins. I moved my car every few hours. No one noticed me. The neighborhood had big houses from the 1910s and '20s and wide sidewalks with big magnolia trees on the curb line; it was built for walking but no one walked, not while I was there, although I saw a few people drive in or out in Mercedes and BMWs.

Mostly April sat on the sofa watching movies. And sleeping. And crawling to the bathroom on her hands and knees to vomit because she was too weak and in too much pain to stand. She also spent a lot of time crying.

No one came to see her. I didn't think anyone called, either. Her parents were dead. She didn't have any kids. She had a sister but the sister was busy or maybe they weren't close or maybe the sister, like everyone else, got sick of this woman and her never-ending problems and just stopped calling.

I watched her for two days. After the second day I went home and spent some time on the internet, putting things together. The husband's first wife had died fifteen years ago in a hotel room in Disneyland. Heart attack. His name was Jack Sweet. Hers, the first wife's, the dead wife's, was Evelyn Sweet, née Evelyn Schwartz.

The next day I asked Lisa if she would meet me at her office. She said she would and she did. I told her I thought the wife was sick. Really sick. I suspected the husband was poisoning her. I told her I suspected he'd murdered his first wife and now he was murdering this woman, too.

I asked Lisa if I could look into it for one more day before we went to the police. We both knew why I was asking: The police had limits on what they could do. By the time they got a warrant, April could be dead. I asked for one day because more could put Lisa's PI license in jeopardy. You were supposed to bring stuff like this to the cops right away. You didn't want to provoke the CBSIS, the mysterious and occulted organization in charge of Lisa's license—and mine.

Lisa listened carefully, asked all the right questions, and then asked some more. She asked to see all the stuff about the first wife online and I showed her, along with some medical records I'd dredged up. Thirty-five years old, no high blood pressure, no history of heart trouble.

"No," Lisa said. "No no no. This is what we'll do." She wanted to go to April right now, this very moment. Get her out of that house and someplace safe. I pointed out we might lose valuable proof, and a conviction, if we did that. Lisa said she didn't care about a conviction. She cared about April. I saw something in Lisa I hadn't seen before: a violent, angry, protective love of women. I was fine with her plan, and that was what we did.

We got in her car and drove to April's house. We rang the bell a bunch of times and she didn't answer. We talked about maybe coming back later, but neither of us moved. We just stood there, ringing the bell again every thirty seconds or so. The door had two glass panels.

After a while I started to feel sick and anxious. "We've got to get in that house," I said. Lisa agreed. In the garden I picked up the heaviest rock I could lift, carried it back up the stairs, and tried to break the glass with it. I couldn't. Lisa, who was stronger, took the rock and broke the window in two big cracks. I reached through the broken glass to unlock the locks and we pushed the door open and went in.

The house was dead quiet inside. Not a good sign. I looked at Lisa and I knew we were both thinking the same thing: that maybe we'd fucked up, the biggest fuck-up of all, and we were too late. We split up and went through the house.

I found April in the bathroom. She was on the floor, messy with blood and vomit and fluids I couldn't and didn't want to name. She was alive. Unconscious, but alive.

The ambulance came fast and the cops slightly less fast. Lisa and I both knew how to deal with authority and we didn't have any trouble. I didn't exactly lie but I played down how sure I'd been. I made it seem like I was just starting to have doubts about it all when Lisa and I came to talk to April.

Lisa had some sterile sample/evidence bags in her car. After the cops and the ambulance left we took a sample of the effluvia on the bathroom floor. I also took samples of the water and whatever was in the fridge. Lisa videoed me taking the samples for integrity's sake. The cops would do their part, but we only trusted ourselves.

I called April's sister, June. This was what I knew about April and June: They were "friends" on a website called Friendster but never spoke there. June lived nearby, in El Cerrito, but according to her obsessive check-ins hadn't made it up to Sacramento in at least a few years. June liked restaurants that served exotic-to-her food in rough-for-her neighborhoods. Her politics were described as "the worst nightmare of the religious right." I wondered how she knew what the religious right dreamed of, or how they even existed at all—here in Northern California the religious right were more of a convenient belief to define yourself against than a real force, like Mercury retrograde, or archons. But that didn't stop the good, gullible people of the Bay Area from designing their lives around the imagined nightmares of their others.

I called June. I'd made dozens of similar calls and the first minute or two was always hard.

"I'm calling about your sister—she's OK, but she's in the hospital," I said. Something prompted me to add: "She could really use a sister now. A friend."

June's response was a long sigh followed by: "What did April get herself into now?"

"Well," I said, feeling my face turning hot. "Actually. Actually. She didn't *get herself* into anything. She's very sick, and we're not entirely sure what's going on, but the police are investigating her husband. He might have done something to make her sick. He might have hurt her."

There was another big sigh. "Well, he's always been, you know," June said.

"No," I said. "I don't know. What has he always been?"

"An asshole," June said. "She's always gone for the assholes."

Right. Hard to imagine where April got the idea that she should surround herself with assholes with no respect for her.

Finally June took down the hospital information and promised that she would visit April. I wondered what kind of a fucking world this was where you had to convince someone that their own sister being poisoned nearly to death wasn't her fault.

But what did I know? Maybe April had done horrible things to June. Maybe there'd been a childhood of fear and torture. The victim and victimizer don't stay in their roles; they switch in and out, shedding their skins like snakes as they grow.

When I got off the phone with June I felt defeated by the whole world, or rather, the people in it: by our stupidity, our inability to learn, our eagerness to play the roles of Helpless Victim and Cruel Bully.

Lisa and I sent the samples to a lab. Three weeks later the results came back. Antifreeze, served a little bit at a time over weeks.

April recovered. Mostly. After a few weeks in the hospital she was able to live on her own again. Her liver and kidneys were beat up but they'd hold for now. Of course, she got everything she wanted in the divorce, and got to stay in the house.

I went to see April when she was back home. It was a few days before Christmas. Her house looked like a department store, full of expensive and impersonal gold decorations that no one had ever loved.

She was alive. That was about all you could say. She was alive and she had some money. I'd been kind of hoping the sister would be there with her, or a friend would have appeared. None did.

"I don't know what to say," April said. "You saved my life. I can't thank you enough."

But she didn't sound thankful. She sounded like she was reading from a bad script. She didn't seem happy to be alive. She was still in pain and had no energy. And she knew the person she'd once loved most in the world, the person she'd once trusted above all others, had tried not just to divorce her or leave her but end her tenure on this earth. Erase her until no mark of her, or by her, was left.

I sat in her uncomfortable living room and we talked for a while. Mostly about health stuff. I got that even before all this she'd been a hypochondriac, bouncing from holistic nutritionist to iridologist to chiropractor. I believed those methods could help people. Just not people like us.

"Please don't take this the wrong way," April said.

"But I feel like your energy has a giant crack in it. A giant crack you need to fix."

I knew she was right. I looked at April and saw her own crack. But neither of us would be easily fixed.

Lisa and I kept working on April's case. We didn't ask for money but eventually April started paying us, including a fat check for services rendered thus far, namely saving her life. Although no one, least of all April, seemed to know what it was being saved for.

Lisa handed the check to me, something she didn't have to do. Fifty grand. Lately, I found myself astounded by every act of decency. We'd split fees on the case going forward. It was more than fair.

Eventually the police verified, legally and admissibly, what we'd found through illegal and surreptitious means: antifreeze. April got groceries delivered, and arranged the deliveries for early in the morning, so they'd be there when she woke up. The husband injected it in her food while it waited for her on the porch. Only the sweets: fruit, bread, juice. All that effort—buying the needle and syringe and figuring out the dose and the timing and stalking her house from dawn to delivery—all that instead of just walking away. Just saying goodbye.

Jack Sweet was arrested, tried, found guilty, and sentenced to life, with parole possible in ten years.

Lisa and I kept working. We found out more about the first wife, talked to her family and friends. We went to the police and the DA and got everyone to agree to exhume her body.

She'd also been poisoned.

Jack Sweet was tried again, found guilty again, and sentenced to life again, this time with no possibility of parole.

♠

I checked on April once in a while. She got better physically. But she seemed unmoored from life, as if the only thing keeping her here was the lack of a current taking her away.

I remembered an episode of *Bewitched* where Darrin saved a Japanese businessman from jumping off a bridge. Reached out and grabbed him, whether he wanted it or not. But because he'd saved the man's life, Darrin was now responsible for this businessman for the rest of both of their lives, a supposed Japanese custom.

But April wasn't a TV character. She didn't need me in her life, and after six or nine months she stopped returning my phone calls.

I used every trick I knew to find the episode of

Bewitched. I thought maybe if I could watch it again, some memory of insight of how to help people would be shaken loose. But I never found it, and if the best detective in the world couldn't find it, it probably never existed at all, and no further insight came.

The crime was solved, but I knew the case wasn't closed.

That would take another twenty years.

♠

Life went on. I built up my practice and my reputation, such as it was, and forgot about April. Until, nearly ten years after I'd first met her, she called me. She had to remind me who she was.

"April Haversmith," she said. "You saved my life? Antifreeze?"

I was in my loft in San Francisco, drinking coffee with a big splash of amaretto for breakfast, feeling exhausted after the Case of the Broken Sparrow. Sometimes it seemed like no one won in life. Not really. Once an old homicide cop told me that he felt no better solving a murder than not. "You just ruined a bunch more lives," he said—he meant the lives of those who loved the killer, happiness now forever lost—"and you didn't bring anyone back."

It didn't bring much satisfaction. On bad days it all looked like an elaborate pantomime, a Punch and Judy show with nothing behind the curtain. People pretended to fall in love so they could act out the motions of being in love, like they'd seen in movies and read about in books, but they forgot it was a game. Hey, guess what, I like stripes too. Hey, I like all those things at Pottery Barn too. Hey, I'm mad at this person, great idea, I'll murder them. And then I'll fuck up and get caught and someone else will jump up to play the part tomorrow, as if it had never been played before. As if we'd all decided to put on a little amateur show and gotten trapped in it, forgotten we were acting and mistaken it all for real. As if we'd forgotten that nothing on this earth was worth killing for.

It was a fucking merry-go-round. Shooting, stabbing, poisoning, ripping each other's throats out. And more often than not, once they got what they'd once wanted, they realized what a terrible mistake they'd made. When the cops were on their way to arrest the killer on the Case of the Broken Sparrow, he suddenly understood. He looked at me, face white.

"Why did I do it?" he asked.

"I don't know," I told him. He started to weep. I held his hand until the police came.

I tried not to think about it. I thought about it anyway.

"Sacramento?" April said.

"Right," I said. "Sorry. How are you?"

"I think," she said. "I think I need a detective again. I think my sister is stealing from me."

It wasn't the kind of case I would ordinarily take at this point in my life, but I still felt obligated to April, like Darrin and the businessman, so I drove up to Sacramento later that week. April had sold the house where her husband tried to kill her. Now she lived in a condo in a big new soulless development. It was near Christmas again. On her coffee table was a collection of plaster fruit in a bowl, painted gold, bought in a store.

April was drinking a lot of wine. I didn't blame her. She explained it all to me; there was a family trust that her sister, June, managed. But April noticed that it had been shrinking, and she suspected that June had been, in a roundabout way, slowly transferring assets out. April confronted June, but June had lied, and now April didn't know what to do.

"My father left us that trust. It isn't just the money," April kept saying. "It isn't just the money. My father wanted me to have it. He loved me. I need to know the truth."

I didn't know exactly how to sort it all out, but I knew how to find people who could. First was a forensic accountant in Las Vegas I knew we could trust. Next he connected us with a lawyer who understood all the ins and outs of real estate and trusts and all the other quicksand the archons made to trap us here.

A few months and nearly a hundred thousand dollars in legal and accounting fees later, it was proven: June was indeed out to fuck April. April convinced her lawyers not to go to the DA. "I just want it to be over," April kept saying. "I don't want to screw her over. I just want to live."

April started to sob.

"I just want to be left alone," she choked out between sobs. "I just want everyone to leave me alone."

Everyone settled on a mediation to work out the money, after which the sisters would never have to speak again, and likely never would.

I was in in a conference room with April and June and the lawyers when it all ended. The lawyers worked out penalties for June and protection for April and they reached an agreement to split what was left, in April's favor, so April could have complete control of her share. April's lawyers, a man and a woman, looked disgusted with June. Everyone looked disgusted with June. As much as possible, April's lawyers squeezed in little cracks: "When the party engaged in theft, for which her sister generously declined to press charges…" "When the opposing party siphoned money from their shared account…" "If opposing counsel had participated in discovery…"

Everyone looked at June with disgust except April. April looked at June through it all as if she was asking for forgiveness, maybe for having been born, maybe for revealing the family secret that June was a terrible and selfish woman.

June looked straight ahead the whole time, eyes barely blinking, her face pure rage.

At the end of it, I visited April in her condo in Sacramento again. Now she couldn't stop crying.

"I have no one," she said. "No one."

I didn't know what to say. I wasn't close to many people, but there were a few I trusted. My doctor, Nick; my assistant, Claude. That was a universe away from *no one.*

Part of the trust, a part she'd won in the settlement, was a small house on Bodega Bay.

"I don't want to go to Bodega Bay alone," she said. "I don't know what to do."

I stayed with her for a while and then I left. I went on a little bit of a bender with my friend Tabitha that night, and a few days later I realized Christmas had passed by in a fog of ketamine and amaretto. I hiked up to the redwoods in Oakland, looking for the Red Detective.

Finally I found him deep in an amanita patch, and we stayed up late in the night talking, and when dawn came I felt a little better.

I thought about April. I wished I had something for her. I didn't.

Another ten years went by.

♠

I was almost fifty. As usual, I had nothing to do for Christmas. Some years on the holidays I would drive around and give away money to people on the street, which some years I could afford and some I couldn't. Now there were so many people on the street in San Francisco I'd be out of cash before I drove a block.

I'd been in Los Angeles for most of the year. I was tired of the cold and tired of what San Francisco had become: a laboratory for the rich where the poor were experimented on. Self-driving cars and fentanyl and ten grand a month for a spot to lay your head. The room-by-the-week hotel I'd once stayed at had been bought by a sex club/Ponzi scheme and then a tech start-up/Ponzi scheme and then a nonprofit housing/Ponzi scheme and was now a room-by-the-week hotel again. I stopped in and asked once, out of curiosity. It was 2k a week, and half the rooms were empty.

"There's just not that many people who can afford it," the kid at the desk said. He was maybe thirty, clean-cut and Midwestern and smart and sad. "I tried letting this lady stay in one of the empty rooms, but the owners got mad at me. I had to sign something saying I wouldn't do it again. That I could go to jail."

Then later that night I ran into him at Buddha Bar and we slept together. I still saw him around the neighborhood sometimes.

On Christmas Day I was on my sofa watching *Hart to Hart* on TV when Hans Richler called. Hans had been friends with my old boss, Constance Darling, and he'd tried to be my friend over the years. I couldn't think of a worse job. Hans was a wealthy man, and though he wasn't a detective, we were both admirers of the great, long-dead detective Jacques Silette.

"Claire!" he said with excitement. Hans was from Austria and spoke with a thick accent. "I go on my way to Las Vegas and the plane, she have a problem, and so we stay in San Francisco. This is perfect, yes? I spend Christmas with you. I can take you some places?"

Hans would have preferred to go somewhere upscale and expensive for dinner, but it was Christmas, and the swell spots were either closed or booked solid. Instead we went to the vegan Chinese restaurant around the corner from my apartment. Hans, a good sport, loved it. It was run by a lady who called herself the Enlightened Mistress. I wasn't sure if she ran a cult or was just a little self-aggrandizing. She had a TV on the wall that played loops of her speaking in Chinese with subtitles tickertaping across the bottom of the screen. Her hair was long and white-blonde and she wore a gold dress. When she talked she held her hands out to her sides in a kind of gesture of religion or belief or hope.

Hans and I caught up. He had big stories about a love affair in Tulum and a rare bottle of wine lost and found in Cuba. But after his stories, he seemed to collapse a little. I wondered if there'd really been an issue with the plane at all, or if he just wanted to see a friend. Hans tried to live an honest life, but all that money made it hard.

I was never smart enough to lie to rich people. But I also didn't know what to say to Hans. Adventure would only get you so far in life. He knew that, and didn't need me to say it out loud. He'd looked for something better and, in some ways, found it, in Silette's work. But *better* wasn't always enough.

The jewel in the lotus is yours, the Enlightened Mistress said on Enlightened Mistress TV. *All you need to do to find it is to give it away.*

After dinner we walked down Stockton Street. The

street was growing dark and cold and a handful of people walked quickly east or west, heads down, trying to get through another day, Christmas be damned. A couple of homeless people hung around in doorways or by the curb, trying to stay out of the wind.

"Come on," Hans was saying. "I know an absinthe bar, they'll open for us. We'll have some fun."

I was about to say *sure*, even though I'd had enough absinthe for three lifetimes. And then, for some reason, a beat-up Hyundai pulling up to the curb caught my eye.

A woman got out of the Hyundai. She had long gray hair, and wore worn leggings under a cheap puffer coat and decent winter boots. Two of the homeless people came to greet her and give her a hand as she got out of the car, popped the trunk, and took out a bunch of meals in plastic containers as people started lining up by the car.

I didn't recognize the woman until I heard her voice.

"Claire," she said.

It was April. She looked completely different, not just because ten years had passed. Her face was bright and something was clear about her; some kind of film had been cleaned away.

She hugged me.

"April—" I began, but she stopped me.

"First, work," she said. "Then talk."

April looked at Hans, and some strange knowledge passed between them that I would never fully understand. April put us to work handing out meals, first on Stockton, then in Washington Square, then down by the wharves. Hans did as he was told and, for a rich man, was surprisingly good at actually working. A lot of people on the street knew April and seemed to respect her fiercely. When a man by Washington Square tried to reach into the trunk of her car for an extra meal, three people jumped to her defense, ready to fight for her. Hans, too, to my surprise, was ready to fight. But with surprising grace, April calmed everyone down and gave the thief an extra meal for later and left everyone safe and feeling OK. In fact, she seemed to leave every person she encountered a little soothed and a little better off from their moment together—a joke there, a sweet word here, a few handshakes and embraces.

As the sun came up, April drove us to a camp on Valencia, Hans in the passenger seat, me squeezed in the back.

"After I saw you last," April said, "I decided to kill myself. So I began by setting everything in order, and giving everything away. First, I set everything up for my sister to get our father's money. After all, it meant more to her than I did. Then I gave my ex-husband's mother everything from his estate. It meant the world to her, as you know. And then, after that, I actually didn't want to die so much anymore. I felt better. So I just kept giving everything away. I gave my condo to this woman in the neighborhood, Janice, who'd lost her house. She was sleeping in her car. I gave my car to my housekeeper—of course she wasn't my housekeeper anymore, but we traded cars.

"I moved to the house on Bodega Bay. Now I knew why I was alive: not to try to hold on to things, but to give them away. My whole life, I'd had it all backwards. When I had everything—money, a husband, a family—I had nothing. But once I had almost nothing, I had everything."

I rolled down the window and looked out to the dirty street beyond. When we stopped at the camp on Valencia and Sixteenth, I was tired, and I told them I was going home. Hans protested, and insisted on multiple hugs and promises before he would let me go. April just smiled at me—but before I got into a cab, she hugged me too, and whispered a *thank you* in my ear.

I didn't go home; I went to an after-hours club I knew in an unused office building downtown, where I gave myself a nosebleed and took two pills I shouldn't have and thirty hours later woke up in the bartender's sunny bedroom in Oakland, with the bartender and her neighbor standing above me yelling my name. I wasn't waking up and they were worried I was dying, although not worried enough to inconvenience anyone by calling 911. I didn't die. I threw up a few times in the bathroom and left and took a hot shower at home and spent the rest of the week on a case and forgot, when it was solved, that I'd ever not felt exactly this: the crisp and clear beauty of a solution. Two weeks later I was in the same after-hours, wiping blood off my upper lip in the bathroom again.

♠

Another three years passed. It was the end of a long night after the end of a long case. I was high and a little drunk and I drove around the city because I had no one to celebrate with and nothing else to do and didn't want to go home alone.

Driving by a homeless camp on the Haight, I saw something that made me stop.

I pulled over to look more closely.

It was Hans. With him was April. They were handing out food and water to the camp from the back of April's car again, laughing and joking with the residents as they did. Hans and April were beloved. Hans's skin was dark from time in the sun, and his hair was long and wild, but I recognized his big laugh from twenty feet away. When the food and water were passed out, April talked to a pregnant woman, handing her some papers and pamphlets, and Hans sat on a bench with one of the men, smoking a cigarette and laughing. Hans pulled a silver flask out of his pocket and handed it to the man, and they passed it back and forth as they laughed.

The Case of the Jewel in the Lotus was closed.

My case was still open. I drove home alone.

THE END

ONE-MINUTE MYSTERY: THE CASE OF THE RAZOR'S EDGE BETWEEN LIFE AND DEATH

Some days in San Francisco the clouds dropped down just low enough to make everything gray and calm and dotted with cool rain and you could believe that there was some softness in the world. But those same clouds could also convince you that life was an eternal twilight, and that you would never see the sun again and, maybe, that you didn't deserve to.

It was one of these clouded days in San Francisco when Claire DeWitt, the best detective in the world, was eating dumplings in soup with rice and oolong tea in the vegan Chinese restaurant on Stockton Street. With Claire was her assistant, Claude. Claude was looking at his tofu hot pot with a skeptical eye.

This restaurant was four blocks away from the apartment where Claire lived and worked on a short curved alley off of Washington Street. There were at least four better restaurants between Claire's home and the vegan restaurant, but Claude liked this place, and Claude rarely asked for concessions or advantages. Claire knew she was a difficult boss, and an even more difficult friend—especially now, since the Case of the Broken Sparrow had laid them both low. So: the vegan restaurant.

"What?" said Claire, noting Claude's skeptical eye.

"It smells different," said Claude, looking at his hot pot. "I'm skeptical."

Claire sniffed the mysterious dish, and soon had a skeptical eye herself.

"It smells weird," she said. "It smells sour. Send it back."

"I don't do that," Claude said. "I've never done that."

"I don't understand why you don't think you deserve better food," Claire said, with a bit of an edge. Claire was tired, physically and spiritually, and a thought passed through her mind: *If everyone would just say what they wanted, we wouldn't be in this fucking mess*—the fucking mess being this world and the people in it—but almost as soon as the thought came, she knew it wasn't true, and let it go back wherever it came from. Claude's reticence to cause a scene—a scene by Claude's standards—was not related to the inability of the killer in the Case of the Broken Sparrow to know himself and his true desire.

Claire and Claude continued to discuss the hot pot nonetheless. Around the room were seven other patrons: a thirty-ish mother and her five-ish daughter, eating steaming bowls of wonton soup as the daughter told the mother about a special star she'd gotten in school for drawing; Fred and Sue Huong, an older couple Claire vaguely knew from around the neighborhood (as Claire had often suspected, Fred and Sue Huong loathed Claire; they thought she was a gentrifier and were not entirely wrong); and a young couple with tearstained faces and fragile hope, renewing their coupledom after a heartbreak.

And a woman sitting alone. Later, Claire and Claude would learn her name was Madeline. Madeline had two plates in front of her. On one plate was a lean slice of carrot cake with cream cheese frosting. On the other plate was a fat square of chocolate cake with chocolate frosting.

"How does everything I do," Claude said, frustration in his voice, "translate into some *referendum*, some opportunity for you to hone in on my supposed—"

But Claude stopped talking, because he noticed that Claire had stopped listening. Instead, Claire was staring at the woman with two desserts.

Claude followed Claire's eyes to see what she saw. The woman, Madeline, was around fifty. She had brown and gray hair to her shoulders in no particular style. She wore a T-shirt that had once been a real color but was now almost-blue-verging-on-gray, a baggy black cardigan, and a pair of ill-fitting black pants, tight in the waist and loose in the hips. On the table was a hardcover mystery novel which she did not read. The last things Claire noticed were Madeline's thin socks and her exhausted sneakers.

Claude looked at her again. Madeline was gathering up her book and paying her check. An idea started to form, wordlessly, in Claude's mind…

But before the idea could get too far, Claire stood up, walked to Madeline's table, and sat down across from her.

Claire leaned over and whispered something to Madeline. Madeline didn't say anything for a long, hard moment. Her face changed from amazement to anger to embarrassment to a kind of rough and bitter grief. Then she started to cry.

Claire reached across the table and took Madeline's hands.

"I don't know what I'm going to do," Madeline said, still crying.

"You're starting again," Claire said. "Right now. Right in this moment. You're starting again."

"I don't know how," Madeline said.

"You're already doing it," Claire said.

"OK," Madeline said, face and voice both broken and hopeful, as if admitting a joyful defeat. "OK."

The Case of the Razor's Edge Between Life and Death was closed.

What was the mystery, and how did Claire solve it?

SOLUTION

Claire knew Madeline was going to leave the restaurant, walk to the Golden Gate Bridge, and jump, ending her own life.

While discussing the emotional realities around the hot pot situation with Claude (which he incorrectly imagined to be projections), Claire observed that Madeline was wearing a gold necklace around her neck that was entirely out of character with the rest of her outfit. Claire ran through possibilities in her head, skipping through the options like a ball bouncing on a roulette wheel: did she steal the necklace? No, she'd have sold it. Gift? Sure, but why keep it, when it isn't her style and is worth some cash? And then the roulette wheel slowed and slowed until the ball landed on: *mother*. Her mother had died and left her the necklace. That's a piece of jewelry you wouldn't sell. Her mother had died and, considering that Madeline was still wearing this necklace that wasn't her style, likely recently. But while the necklace was worth money, Madeline's clothes were inexpensive, and her book was from the library. A rich mother plus a poor daughter added up to not a great relationship. Not a great relationship usually meant a painful and complicated death for those left behind. Then Claire noticed Madeline's shoes: thin canvas sneakers, despite the damp cold outside. Madeline had woken up that morning, in the wet cold of the San Francisco Bay, and decided she wasn't worth keeping warm.

The last clue was what Madeline had ordered: two desserts, nothing else, but she ate them with no joy, as if she were—and she was—forcing down her last meal.

Claire knew, better than many, just how brutal and humiliating life can be. Some days it feels like people exist just to break your heart, and other days and other people exist just to pour salt in the broken flesh; sometimes it feels like entire months, years, whole decades exist just to hurt us like it's their fucking hobby.

Claire put all this together in her head with ever-increasing urgency, and she began to worry. Claire rarely worried, usually choosing to feel anger or annoyance instead. But she worried now. What if this woman ended her one precious experience of this incarnation because Claire failed to prevent her? What if, because Claire fucked up, this woman ended her life thinking the world had just let her go? Just recently, in the middle years of middle age, Claire had earned a sense of being tethered to the earth by her communion with others—both specific others and general others, living others and dead. She was glad she had lived to experience this, and didn't want this woman to leave life without it. Our own heartbreaks and failures do not absolve us of the obligation to save others.

Claire walked to Madeline's table, sat down, and confronted her. You know that part. You just read it. Claire hoped that this very act would be enough to startle Madeline into seeing that the world was a strange and mysterious place. A stranger with a mysterious message—who could walk away from a thing just when it was starting to get interesting?

It worked. A mystery was a good reason to stay alive, and Madeline's life was therefore to be kept, at least for a while longer, and not thrown away.

As to what Claire whispered in Madeline's ear, I can't say. No one knows. If I knew the right words to keep everyone alive, the world would look very different than it does now, and I would keep everyone safe, forever. But I trust that if you ever need to save my life, you'll know what to say, and the right words will drip from your lips like a flower's nectar to a hummingbird's tongue. Maybe it already happened, and you've already saved me. Maybe the only reason we're here is because we already saved each other. Thank you.

The Case of the Razor's Edge was closed.

THE END

THE CASE OF THE BLOOD ON THE SNOW

Father Billy was getting old. His hair had gone from black to silver to white to yellow. His skin, once taut and firm across his high Harry Dean Stanton cheekbones, had sunk down to hollow out his eyes and face.

I'd met Father Billy on a case. A case like the one that had put me in the hospital this time. That case put me in the hospital too—one of my first extended stays. I don't know how long I was in this time before he came to see me. It would be months before I got the chronology of those first few weeks sorted out, and some of it is still hazy.

He'd come a long way to see me. Maybe because he knew I needed it. Father Billy Finn was a New Yorker of the type they didn't make anymore. Born in Gowanus to an Irish-Italian-Polish-Puerto-Rican family of five kids: three dock workers, back when there was still work on the docks; one priest, Father Billy; and the baby, Angie. Mother Finn raised the kids, kept the house spotless, and cooked breakfast, lunch, and dinner for the family. When the kids got a little older she got a part-time job as a cashier in a diner in Brooklyn Heights, just outside the A train, to "keep busy." Their father was a dock worker who also sometimes drove a cab and also sometimes helped out with the numbers in Carroll Gardens.

But in the end all their busyness and work and protections didn't add up to much for the Finns. The docks closed. Most of the boys went into corrections or security, where they met a whole new level of brutality and the drugs to find relief from it. Father Billy lost the Brooklyn parish he and his family had put every spare penny into for a hundred years when the Church shut it down, although he was given a new one in Manhattan. And Angie—Angie's long, sad story is for another day.

When I woke up in the hospital, for some reason I wasn't surprised to see Father Billy sitting next to me.

I sat up. I was alive. I wasn't sure if that was a great thing. A doctor came in to explain to me that I was fucked, but could likely be reassembled. I'd been shot, for the second time, and the bullet had gone clear through my upper left shoulder, far from my heart but through a thick web of muscle and nerve and tendon, chipping my collarbone on the way in.

The doctor left. Billy took my hand.

"Now, I want to tell you a story about Mary," he said. "Not that Mary. This Mary was a prostitute down on Allen Avenue. You remember. We had the van that would go out with condoms and needles and some food. You remember that. There was a woman who worked with me on that—Sister Martha. She was one of those hard nuns, you know, made of rock and bones. Scared the hell out of the other nuns, and you should've seen her with the kids! The women on the street were scared of her too, at first. But most of them warmed up to her once they came to see what she was about. No big soft heart under that tough exterior. She was hard all the way through. You could lean on her all you wanted and she'd never fall down. That's a rare and beautiful woman. One with no softness at all.

"So Mary was one of the women working down on Allen Avenue, and the first time Sister Martha approached Mary to see what she might need, Mary spit in Martha's face. Mary didn't like Catholics very much, obviously, and especially not the clergy. She had good reason, too, as it was a priest who'd ruined her life, taken everything from her, all of her trust and her faith and her health, and no one believed a word from her about it. Her family came to hate her and she left home very young, couldn't find any kind of work, and ended up just where we met her. She lived in a little hotel on the Bowery. The people there, they had a little bit of a community—we knew many of them in the hotel, spent a lot of time there. So she had a little bit of a home, and some friends, which is more than many have. But still not very much.

"Now most of the women, they were happy to see us, happy to take some hot coffee and some supplies, happy to talk for a minute to someone who didn't want anything from them. But Martha goes up to Mary and starts her little talk about is she hungry, what does she need, and Mary spits right at her. Says, you ever talk to me again I'll cut that fucking smile right off your face. So Martha says, OK, I'll keep my face, God bless you, and takes off.

"Now these women, just to paint the picture, they didn't look like the streetwalkers in movies. They didn't have fancy clothes and wigs and high heels. Mary was small, she had dark hair. Bad luck had taken its toll on her. Barely thirty and she used a cane to walk—nerve damage from the drugs. Most of the time she just wore jeans and a thin little coat and sneakers.

"These women weren't so young, and their services were not expensive. A lot of scars. A lot of limps. And a lot of predators preying on them. They were people who were left behind by the world, and for a violent man, it was really just a playground. The women would get beaten, raped, killed, and sometimes, many times, just disappear. All the worst impulses men had, this was where they could carry them out. Thanks to Jesus, sometimes we could be there to help when the women were hurt.

"But there was a lot of fun, too, believe it or not. People were friends. They made families. We made some mistakes—plenty of mistakes—but I like to think, I hope, we helped a bit too.

"But Mary, she didn't want our help. A few years went by and Mary still wouldn't have anything to do with us. Maybe she was just as tough as Sister Martha. Hard all the way through. If we got close to Mary, even by acci-dent, she'd start spitting and cursing all over again.

"Now Sister Martha, you could see she worried over Mary. She knew better than to try to talk to her, of course—she wanted to keep her face! But every once in a while I'd catch Martha just staring at Mary. Just watch-ing her. And every year Mary got thinner, and more exhausted, and more beat up by life. Martha would try to give one of the other women a sandwich or a cup of soup or some candy to give Mary, and tell her not to say where it came from. But somehow Mary always knew. Mary would take that sandwich and very slowly, very carefully, piece by piece, throw it onto the ground and grind it down into the gutter, looking right at us the whole time. She'd rather go hungry than take even a little bit of food we had touched. And who could blame her?

"But Martha, in her own way, never stopped trying to look after Mary. She would look in at the hotel and make sure Mary's bill was paid. She'd leave some extra clothes, give them to the other women, and hope they'd make their way to Mary.

"Then one day, just before Christmas, one of the other women comes running in the van, all worked up. She says Mary got in a car with someone wrong—one of the girls recognized the car, but only when it was too late, when they were already driving away. Said the man had almost killed her, but she got lucky and got out just in time.

"Of course Martha jumped into action. I promise you, if Martha had known how to find it, she would have gone right to that car herself. She wasn't scared of anything. But we didn't know where to go. I had a friend on the force, an officer whose aunt was a Sister. So I called him up and told him everything and Martha begged, literally begged him, to help her look for Mary. So he came around and picked her up and they drove all the usual places. But it started to snow, and snow hard, and the desk sergeant called the officer in, so Martha came back to the van. Usually we would've been done for the night by then, but of course we weren't going home. Not till we found Mary. We drove around until the snow got too bad to drive. Then Martha and me put on our coats and gloves and everything we could find to go out and look for Mary ourselves.

"Now, one thing you have to understand is that New York was different back then. The streets weren't so crowded like they are now. In bad weather you could walk for blocks without seeing another person. So out goes Martha in her black habit and her long black coat in the snow, over a foot of it by then, looking down every block on the Lower East Side for Mary, me tagging along behind her.

"Many years later I found out something I didn't know at the time—Martha had, or used to have, two older sisters. And both became addicts, and both died on the street, just like the women on Allen Avenue. And both died alone.

"We walked and we walked and we walked, Martha and me. My fingers and toes burned with frostbite. And then finally, just before the sun came up, we saw something red and dark in the snow, down at the end of a little alley almost in Chinatown.

"We rushed over and oh my God, was it horrible.

Poor Mary was all cut and beat and blood was pouring out of her. She couldn't even scream. I thought there was just a few breaths left in her. I ran off to find a payphone to call for help and Martha stayed with Mary. For some reason I remember so clearly how it felt to run on those burning cold feet, how adrenaline took me over. Funny the things you keep. I went and I called 911 and then I called the precinct direct and I don't know who else. When I'd called everyone I could think of, I ran back to Martha and Mary.

"Mary was still lying on the ground, bleeding so much you couldn't even think of what to do. Martha sat beside her, covered in blood, trying to do something about all those horrible cuts. Martha had taken off her coat and put it over Mary and now it was all bloodsoaked, too. And I heard Martha whispering to Mary, whispering over and over, 'Please, Mary. Please, just let me hold your hand. Please, just let me warm you up a little. Let me help you.'

"And then, with her last little bit of strength, Mary put her hand out in the snow, and let Sister Martha hold it. Martha took Mary's hand and warmed it up, and got closer, just a little bit at a time, as Mary would allow, trying to keep Mary warm.

"By the time I reached them, the ambulance was

pulling up, and Martha had her arms around Mary, trying to keep her alive, all black and white and red in the snow.

"Mary was almost gone. With her last breath, she whispered something in Martha's ear. I don't know what. Martha lay in the snow and held Mary like she was her own child until they took her away.

"The world is mysterious, Claire. Somehow, Mary lived. When I went home that night I had frostbite on the tip of every toe. Kept them all but one—I miss it sometimes. We kept the van going for a while, but then the diocese cut the budget, and some of the parishioners thought we shouldn't be spending our money on that kind of person anyway. Apparently the Church, in its wisdom, had outgrown that.

"Martha went on a silent retreat after that, and after a few months of prayer and meditation, she left the Sisterhood. I lost touch with her after that.

"But a few years later—this was when I was at my parish in the Village, the same one I'm at now—I started hearing rumors about two women in Central Park. I heard from some of them at our kitchen that these two women would go to Central Park every night and minister to the animals. They'd go out there after dark and take care of the raccoons and the pigeons and the squirrels. They made sure the animals were fed, got help for the injured, settled any disputes among them, and read to the animals from the Good Book, of course.

"Of course this was something I had to see, so I started going to the park at night to find them. It was nearly Christmas again, maybe five years after the Christmas when Mary almost died. It took a few nights of looking, but there they were. Two women, all bundled up in secondhand coats and big hats. They were standing out by the lake where people play with the toy boats, the little pond there, and Mary was reading from one of the other good books—the Bhagavad Gita: 'Free from expectations, they perform no sin.' And I swear to God, Claire, around them were all the animals of the park—ducks, swans, hawks, cats, chipmunks, coyotes—all listening to Mary and Martha read. I left without saying a word.

"The next day I started raising hell, and I didn't stop until they let me start up the van again.

"Now I don't know if there's a lesson in that story for you, Claire. If there is, I don't know what it would be. But I felt like telling it, and you're a captive audience.

"Now, be a good girl and go back to sleep. There you go. That morphine is good stuff; enjoy it while you can."

The next time I woke up, I reached out for Father Billy's hand, but he was gone. He'd died of liver cancer five years back.

I went back to sleep for a few more days. When I woke up again, my friend and doctor Nick Chang was there. He smiled when he saw me, and exhaled like he hadn't let his breath out for a month.

"Good to see you," he said. "You almost left us."

"I know," I said. "An ambassador came to meet me."

"Oh yeah?" Nick said. "What'd they say?"

"That I wasn't done yet," I said.

Nick took my hand, and I took his.

THE END

CHOOSE YOUR OWN HEARTBREAK

CHAPTER ONE

♣

Let's say you're a detective.

You are a person living on planet earth. You are old or young, male or female or not, all of those things or none. You may have been a detective for many lifetimes or you just may be discovering this now. You are a good detective, and you solve most of your cases, most of the time. None of this need be true.

Let's say you're a detective.

Let's say your name is Cynthia Silverton. You are female. You are nineteen and you live in a modern suburban ranch home in the town of Rapid Falls with your housekeeper. Your parents were killed in a mysterious accident when you were a small child, just at the border of where your conscious memory begins, causing you to doubt the few memories of them you may have. The date is sometime between 1959 and today. It is neither warm out nor especially cold. You may or may not be a fictional character, but that's true of all of us.

Or maybe not. Maybe you're a man, thirty-two years old and bright with hope. Maybe you're a woman, fifty-two and tired and always ready to fight.

In any case, let's say you're a detective.

You're a detective, and you are on a very important case. You know the villain well. His name is Hal Overton and as long as you can remember, he has been your villain. You often wonder why Hal Overton has decided to manage his criminal empire from the small town of Rapid Falls, but you always land on *Well, why not?* Everyone has to live somewhere, you guess. And this is a decent place to run a criminal empire from, you guess; sometimes you think the bumbling and alcoholic Sheriff Brown is worse than no sheriff at all. Once or twice a year he has a real, exhausting bender (as opposed to his regular, everyday, excessive drinking) and afterward swears he'll change. He never does. Tonight, for example, you've left four messages for him, and as of now, no return call.

You're at the tail end of the Case of the Liquid Sky. You're sure Overton and his gang are behind the recent influx of opium into Rapid Falls' demimonde, but Overton has taken off with the proof—the shipping receipt that proves one of his minions picked up a cargo shipment of "coffee" from the Amtrak Continental Twilight Express last night. Of course, the bigger mystery is why so many people in Rapid Falls are so heartbroken that they can only find happiness in an opium pipe, and why we've created a world that offers us so few chances for ecstasy, or even ordinary joy, and why we've refused to see that, in addition to ruining each other's lives, we are also each other's only hope—but those are tomorrow's questions. Tonight, there's a crime to solve!

So. Overton. Proof. Receipt. You saw him pick up the paperwork from one of his minions at the café downtown. You had a plan in place, and it seemed like a good plan at the time: wait till Overton leaves the restaurant, catch him off-guard, grab the receipt from the inside pocket of his revolting tweedy overcoat, and get the hell out of there.

But somehow it all got fucked up. You had him cornered in the doorway of the café, ready for your big citizen's arrest—but that fuck Overton is faster than he looks. He faked you out with a left hook and then with his right gave you a lump on your cheek that will turn green and blue tomorrow—more importantly, he got away. While your head was spinning and your vision black, he ran faster than you thought possible and took off south down Main Street. Once he got past the streetlights, you lost track of him.

Fuck. He's gone.

You have a choice.

You can follow Hal Overton and stay on the case. That way lies risk, maybe injury, maybe danger, and definitely heartbreak. Being a detective means having to ask other people for help. And if these last few years have taught you anything, it's that other people will break your heart. They'll let you down, lie to you, attempt to murder you, and worst of all, just when you want them the most, forget about you.

But here you are, with a mystery to solve. Are you willing to risk humiliation, rejection, gunshot, loneliness, stabbing, and heartbreak to solve it?

Or will you go home, put on the TV, heat up a snack, enjoy your intoxicant of choice, and call it a night? Not everything in life is your problem.

You used to live with the rare golden conviction that fate was on your side. Now you're not sure you even have a side, or that there's such a thing as fate.

No one will blame you if you give up now. Go get an apartment somewhere, maybe a condo with a pool.

Fuck Rapid Falls and its abnormally high crime rate. Fuck mysteries and fuck this world and most of all fuck other people. Some people say *Nothing ventured, nothing gained*. Those people don't know what loss is, and you wonder if they've ever really ventured anything at all.

You have a choice: Can you believe that the universe has some adventure left for you? That life—and other people—might still be worth risking another crack in your heart for?

If you say NO, then hey, listen, I don't blame you. People are awful, and so is this fucking world we've made. But going home is not without its own risks: You might wake up in the middle of the night and not know who you are anymore. You might realize with a painful and ugly feeling that you no longer remember what you were so angry about, or why you devoted your life to it. You might realize that instead of letting someone else break your heart, you've broken it yourself.

I'm sorry you let life wear you down, kid, I really am. I know it's hard for you. Guess what? It's hard for everyone. I have no fucking idea what the answer is. All I know is that if you say NO now, I have nothing for you, and you can put this story right down and go on with your life. There's no need to keep reading. Nice speaking with you. Goodbye.

If your answer is YES, welcome to life. You are a detective, and you are on the biggest case of your life, and I wish you luck. You'll need it. Anything can happen and the only thing I can promise you is this: It will hurt. But if you take every risk, and you're willing to fall down and fall down and fall again and still get up, then all of this might, for a moment, be worth it.

Now turn to **Chapter Two**.

CHAPTER TWO

♣

Uh-oh.

You've chased Hal Overton through downtown Rapid Falls, past the bookstore, the hardware store, and the café, all quiet and abandoned and eerie at night.

As a detective, this night-time half-world is your natural habitat; you feel at home here, and as you run down Main Street until it ends, turning into Rural Route 108, you feel alive and you can almost believe that you know yourself now—that you were born for chasing people like Hal Overton; that you are a machine for solving mysteries.

But—here's the uh-oh—Hal turns into the woods right before you get to the South Rapid Falls Business Improvement District (that never improves and does little legit business); aka Twilight Boulevard, aka South Rapid Falls, commonly known as the Bad Strip Mall.

Every town has one. The Bad Strip Mall, which holds the strip club, the tattoo parlor, and the liquor store, is full of Hal Overton's friends.

So: Fuck. You don't know exactly where Hal Overton is, but you know he's close. You want to find him. You do NOT want to be found by him. Both you and Hal Overton are smart and fast and good at this shit: Whoever starts the fight is almost guaranteed to win it.

Hal Overton has often threatened to kill you. You aren't sure if, given the chance, he'll follow through. Maybe. Maybe he'd be content with just taking a limb, or a facial feature.

You look around. With a near-full moon, you are struck by how even the ugliest parts of Rapid Falls have a Lynchian beauty to them: for example, the way the tattered flag in front of the liquor store waves starkly against the moonlit sky. Sometimes Rapid Falls seems like a standardized extract of America, you think, and you wonder if every town has a Hal Overton, and if every town has a detective like you, if you're all just interchangeable players in a play of some sort, but with no audience and to no discernible end…

But while you've been lost in thought, Hal Overton has no doubt been getting closer. You look around again. No obvious weapons appear. You weren't prepared for this late-night adventure and you don't have a gun, or a knife, or even a good rock.

You remember that Joey, the bartender at Rapid Falls All Nude, owes you a favor. On the Case of the Lonely Dancer, you could have ratted him out for holding on to the stolen jewelry for a long hot minute for the fence. But when Joey told you he had a mother with ALS to take care of at home, you promised you would keep his name away from the cops and keep him out of lockup, and you did.

But Joey can also be kind of an asshole sometimes (most of the time, really). And he does all kinds of business with Hal Overton.

So what do you do? Do you believe that the world will catch you if you fall? Do you have faith in the net you've built—or failed to? Do you trust that even though you've often fucked up in life (and sometimes fucked others right along with you), you might have also generated some goodwill?

If you go in to Rapid Falls All Nude to ask Joey for help, go to Chapter Three.

Or do you think it's safer to go it alone? Do you think people are best held at arm's length? Not to be trusted? Is your heart too broken and dented to give anyone another chance to injure it? I don't blame you. Mine is too. Life is too fucking much.

Probably wise. If you keep running, and think you can make it through the night without any help, go to Chapter Eight.

CHAPTER THREE

You've been in Rapid Falls All Nude plenty of times, and every time you're struck by the odd, dim lights and the distinctive smell of alcohol, smoke, and sex. Candy, a dancer you know well enough, is on stage; she nods a hello when you come in. You nod back. The DJ plays Van Halen; you can guess that Aerosmith is next.

Joey is at the bar. He sees you and his mouth curls into a smile. What passes for a smile on Joey, at least. You don't know what to make of it.

"Hey," you say.

"Hey," Joey says. "What're you drinking?"

"Actually," you say, trying to hide your anxiety and your stupid, loathsome need for others. "I could use a favor."

Joey looks serious now.

"You got it," he says.

Eight minutes later you're hiding in the middle of

a maze-like stack of liquor boxes in the basement. Joey says if Hal Overton asks, he hasn't seen you since the Case of the Lonely Dancer. You contain yourself in the box maze, quiet as a good mouse, for twenty minutes. But then you hear two sets of voices coming down the stairs: Joey's, and the raspy, chilling voice of Hal Overton.

Fuck. As they get closer, you hear Hal say, "I thought you said you knew where she was."

Is Joey keeping your secret and lying to Hal? Or did he fuck you, and is he leading Hal right to you?

You've been a detective in this town since before your permanent teeth came in. It's reasonable to think it hasn't been all bad. It's reasonable to think you may have made some friends on the way.

It sounds like Joey is leading Hal to the bathroom on the other side of the basement. If you run now, you *might* be able to sneak past them and make it up the stairs and out the door. *Might*.

Do you trust Joey, and stay? Right on. If so, turn to Chapter Four.

Do you figure he's out to fuck you, and run? Sounds smart. Turn to Chapter Five.

CHAPTER FOUR

♣

You stand as silently and still as you can in Joey's labyrinth of liquor boxes as Joey and Hal clomp toward the bathroom.

You hear Joey explain to Hal, "I don't know where she went. I had the little bitch right here in the bathroom and now she's gone. Fucking detectives. Anyway. Go on up, I'll have Sal make you a sandwich."

"Fuck your sandwiches," Hal Overton says. He sounds angry. "You said she was down here."

"Whattdyou want from me?" Joey says. "I run the All Nude. I'm not a big criminal like you. I don't know how to secure a person. I tied her up with paper towels. I used almost the whole roll. She got away. Come on."

"OK," Hal mutters. "And make the sandwich to go. With mayo."

"Of course," Joey says. "Go upstairs, I'll have it for you in two minutes. On the house."

You hear Hal's limping gait up the stairs.

A moment later, Joey comes through the box maze.

"Wait here," Joey says. "I'll flick the lights once when he's gone."

"Thanks, Joey," you say. "How's your mom?"

"Not good," Joey says, a look of both sadness and pride crossing his face. "But at least she's got me to help her out. Whatever you need, I'm here."

Tears spring to your eyes. Sometimes it seems like life keeps its beauty locked up and hidden away in the strangest, most unlikely places.

Joey turns and heads back upstairs. Eleven minutes later, the lights flick on and off, and with one more meaningful handshake with Joey, you're out of there, free in the cool dark night—but you can bet Hal Overton is still looking for you, and nearby.

Weeks later, you will receive, in the mail, a snapshot of Joey and his mother, Ana, silent and expressionless in her wheelchair, near the beach. You remember that, on the Case of the Lonely Dancer, Joey had told you, holding back tears, that he just wanted to take his mother to see the ocean one last time.

On the back of the photo will be written one misspelled word: *finaly.*

Turn to Chapter Six.

CHAPTER FIVE

♣

So you've decided to try to break free of the basement. Joey, like most humans, just can't be trusted. When you hear Joey and Hal Overton's voices turn echoey in the tiled bathroom, knowing that might provide some decent cover, you run, as swiftly and silently as you can, toward the stairs.

Unfortunately, it doesn't work. While Hal Overton and Joey are looking for you in the bathroom and you're trying to sneak behind their backs to the stairs, Joey turns around and spots you. But before you can react, Joey does something amazing.

"There she is!" Joey says. "Under the sink!"

Joey directs Hal's attention to the cheap particle-board cabinet under the sink—away from you.

You get up the stairs and out of the bar and back on Route 108, safe for the moment—and a little stunned that Joey took such a risk for you.

Weeks later, you will receive, in the mail, a snapshot of Joey and his mother, Ana, silent and expressionless in her wheelchair, near the beach. You remember that, on the Case of the Lonely Dancer, Joey had told you, holding back tears, that he just wanted to take his mother to see the ocean one last time.

On the back of the photo will be written one misspelled word: *finaly.*

Turn to Chapter Six.

CHAPTER SIX

♣

So here you are, on Route 108, alone. At dawn, maybe you can find the alcoholic Sheriff Brown and convince him to lock Hal up for a few days to cool off. But for now, Hal might still be close. And so when a car pulls up beside you, barely rolling, keeping pace, you're sure it's Hal—with a bullet for you.

But before you can run, you hear a strained woman's voice from the car.

"Hey," you hear. "Hey, Cynthia."

You turn around. A beat-up station wagon from twenty years ago, held together by electrical tape and wire hangers, is a few feet away. Driving is Sally McQueen, former clerk at Rapid Falls Liquor Mart, retired manager of Hamburger Hank's, retired mistress of Hank himself, proud caretaker of three feral cat colonies around the edges of Rapid Falls.

At least it's not Hal. But Sally? Really? Nothing against Sally, a lifetime member of Rapid Falls's twilight world of victimless crime. You've crossed paths plenty of times, and you've always liked her. She's just not who you would dream of having on your side in a fight. But she's got a car and can get you out of here and get you safe and you have to admit you need her.

The other problem is that the last time you saw Sally you were, frankly, kind of an asshole. You were hunting down the Clue of the Mercury Dime, which led to the feral cat colony outside the abandoned 7-Eleven off Route 44, and Sally was in the way while you were looking through the store for the titular dime and you rolled your eyes and said something like "Jesus, Sally, can I solve my fucking mystery here?"

Looking back, you were definitely an asshole.

You've wanted to apologize to Sally for months. But an apology now, when you need a favor, will seem fake and opportunistic. Sally deserves better.

You fucked up. What do you do now?

Look, this is just a story. No one knows what the answers are here. All I'm saying is: We have no way out. We're all stuck here with each other. You can loathe other people or love them—they'll be there nonetheless, ruining everything, a constant problem. Maybe the only thing to do is to try to work it out.

Do you get in the car with Sally? If so, turn to Chapter Seven.

Or will you let the fucking misery of it all overwhelm you, and give up trying to make sense of the mess that is other people? Why would Sally forgive you, and why would you want her forgiveness?

Do you tell Sally to keep driving, and go it alone? Yeah, I probably would too. Turn to Chapter Nine.

CHAPTER SEVEN

♣

You get in the car with Sally. Sally's wise to this town and it doesn't take a minute to explain to her what you're up to and what you need. She knows a spot to keep you safe. But first, she needs to feed the cats. She drives you to a family of strays behind the abandoned salt factory on Salt Factory Road.

It's dark. You sit in the passenger seat, which smells like cats and dust and medication.

"Listen," you say, stomach a little shaky. "I've been meaning to say. I was kind of a dick the last time I saw you. I raised my voice, and I acted like a jerk. I just want you to know I'm sorry. You've always been so cool to me."

Sally smiles and waves your regret away.

"Oh honey," she says. "I've seen worse. Don't worry about it. But you're a good kid to say that."

You feel a small influx of relief and shame, in equal

measure. You determine, for the millionth time, to stop being an asshole. Maybe it'll stick this time. Probably not.

"You know," Sally says. "Me and Hal, we go way back. We go back before we were born. See, my great-great-grandmother, Mary Worthington Able, was the first person to live in Rapid Falls."

Of course, you know the story of Mary Worthington Able, the town founder: mystic, escaped slave, philanthropist, seer. Mary Worthington Able saw Rapid Falls in a vision; the town beckoned her from the future, pulling her toward it as she escaped a plantation outside of New Orleans and made her way north. And you did know, dimly, that Sally was one of her descendants.

"But what not a lot of people know," Sally says, "is that Alice Overton, Hal's great-great-grandmother, was the second resident."

You frown. You did not know this. You'd always thought of Hal Overton as a mar in the fabric of Rapid Falls, a mistake to be fixed. Is it possible he's just another thread in the whole? That he belongs here as much as you or Sally?

You wonder, with the feeling of winter light in your eyes, even though it's night: Is it possible you have no enemies at all?

You put the thought aside, finding it strangely uncomfortable.

Together, you and Sally scatter cheap dry cat food around the abandoned parking lot. The cats are howling, ratty, semi-feral monsters. But they seem to know Sally, and they send their tails straight up with joy when they hear her voice. Even cats need people, our original sin.

Done with the cats, you get back in the car together.

"Hey," you say to Sally as you drive around the edge of town. "Is the Liquor Mart open? I could buy us something."

"Nah," Sally says, smiling. "But I bet I got something in the backseat."

Tomorrow you'll find Sheriff Brown and try, yet again, to make him sober up and do his fucking job. For now, you and Sally pull over to the rest stop off Route 44, car hidden behind the Quonset hut, and kill a pint of Jim Beam.

"You know, I've always liked you," Sally says, and for some reason that brings tears to your eyes.

"I've always liked you too," you say to Sally. "I'm so sorry again about being such an asshole."

"Yeah, I'm an asshole too sometimes," Sally says. "Every day I wake up and try to be better. Usually I don't make it. But I try."

Tomorrow, I will try to be better, you tell yourself, internal voice drunk and messy. *Tomorrow, I will try again.*

Sally looks at you and, as if reading your mind, says, "Kid. It's no big deal. I forgive you. You can't be so hard on yourself all the time. You're never gonna get through life alive like that."

You feel tears in your eyes again. Together you see and feel the warm glow of the sun as it rises, prismatic through the Jim Beam bottle. It's tomorrow now. You will try again.

THE END

CHAPTER EIGHT

You're alone now. You walk in the dark woods, lit only by occasional slivers of moonlight, until you reach the oldest tree in Rapid Falls.

Tomorrow, when dawn breaks and you're sure Hal Overton is far off your trail, you can double back to town and enlist the help of the loathsome alcoholic Sheriff Brown. He'll arrest Overton, fuck it up as usual, and Overton'll get out on a technicality a few days later when Judge Schwartz sets him free again. You used to think that one day you'd clean up this town for good. Tonight, you suspect that Hal Overton is as much a part of Rapid Falls as you are.

You climb up a few branches in the oldest tree and find a stable spot to hide for the night. You look at your phone. Two missed calls from Sheriff Brown.

A little fire of anger starts to grow inside you. Fucking

alcoholics are never there when you need them. You call him back.

"Hey, Cynthia," he mutters. You can hear the shame in his voice, and the start of the next day's hangover already creeping in.

"You know I could have used some help tonight," you say. "I'm stuck in a fucking tree. Overton almost killed me."

You know you're right, but the anger in your voice sounds ugly, and you don't like the way it tastes in your mouth. On the other hand, why should you pretend this shit is okay?

"Yeah," Sheriff Brown says. "I think I fell asleep."

Of course that means *passed out*.

"I don't know what to say," you say honestly.

"I know," Sheriff Brown says. "No one does anymore."

You sigh.

"I'm gonna get help," Sheriff Brown says. "I can't go on like this."

You've heard this two dozen times before. But what can you do? You and Sheriff Brown are stuck together. You wish you didn't care about him. But you do. You wish he didn't drink. But he does.

You have a vague but chilling sensation that last night ended just like tonight, and tomorrow will start just like today did. But you push the thought aside. You know it isn't true, but you feel that if you could find the right words, the perfect string of letters, you could cure him. You've known Sheriff Brown your entire life. What is love if not nineteen years of tolerating each other? You search for the magic syllables, the words that will elevate you both out of the awful, unoriginal horror of his addiction. But when you open your mouth, nothing magical comes out.

"Well," you say lamely. "I'm around if you need anything."

"Thanks," he says, shame dripping from the word.

Neither of you has anything else to say, but you stay on the phone anyway.

"Are we OK?" Sheriff Brown finally says.

"Yeah," you say, "I guess. We're OK."

You're not sure if it's true.

No one hangs up. Maybe this, you think, is love: staying on the phone with someone who broke your heart. Sometimes you get to choose your heartbreak; you might as well, you figure, choose to break it for a cause, and so you stay on the phone and listen to Sheriff Brown alternate between silence and tears until your battery dies.

Then you go home, and plug your phone in, and call him back.

THE END

CHAPTER NINE

♣

You're in a meadow in the woods. It's night. Who knows how you got here? Does anyone care? Does it matter? Is anyone keeping track? Are we all just acting in a play with no fucking audience here?

Anyway. Meadow. Night. Overton. You made it, kid, and you made it alone. You have what you wanted: success, on your own terms. You did it your way, alone.

But now you find out the truth: There is no escape from heartbreak. There is no reprieve from caring about other people. At some point (when, exactly?) you stopped letting anyone get close. You thought your solitude would protect you. But now you see: There is no winning this war. Nothing can protect you. A meadow alone is no meadow, and a solitary triumph is a smack in the face.

You sit on the ground, crying, overwhelmed by all the people you've lost: parents;, friends, other detectives, clients, lovers. No one has replaced them as they've gone. How did you get here? How did you get to be your age and have no relationships strong enough to tether you to the earth? Why was it so hard to trust Joey? Or Sally? Or anyone, ever? Why could you only love people who were out of reach? Why was real closeness always tomorrow, never today? Why was love always abstract, never concrete and real?

Sometimes you feel like you could float away, because you will never let anyone love you enough to hold on to you and keep you here.

You lie on the cold damp grass, drowning in self-pity. You've forgotten that you're a glamorous and important detective, always with her guard up, never letting anyone get nearer than you want them to. And so when you sit up and open your eyes, it is with utter fucking shock that you see Hal Overton crouched next to you with a knife in his hand.

But to your surprise, Hal puts the knife down and sits next to you on the cold earth.

"Are you going to kill me?" you say.

"Yes," Hal says. "But not tonight."

Instead, you trade stories about old times when you almost killed each other and the great unsolved crimes of Rapid Falls and Joey and Sally and everyone else you know.

When the night ends, you watch the sun come up over the woods together.

"Do you hear that?" Hal says.

You listen. You hear nothing.

"That," Hal says, "is the sound of everything changing."

"Even me?" you ask.

"Yes," Hal says. "Even you."

THE END

CYNTHIA SILVERTON AND THE CHARNEL HOUSE GROUNDS

"And so," said Cynthia Silverton, world's greatest teen detective, to the assembled crowd of police, shoppers, and crime victims in the PriceSlasher parking lot, "I think we can all see now that the real villain in this case is our beloved grocer Tommy Madison. But what you probably didn't know is that Tommy Madison…"

The svelte teen detective walked over to the balding, portly Tommy Madison and, in one swift gesture, ripped off his face.

The crowd gasped with fear as they saw Cynthia attack, and then gasped again as they saw who was underneath Tommy Madison's lifelike mask: local criminal mastermind Hal Overton!

"Sheriff Brown," Cynthia said, with perhaps a hint of smugness, "I think this one's ready for another arrest!"

But Sheriff Brown, along with everyone else, was running for cover. Hal Overton had suddenly manifested, in a cloud of white and strange-smelling smoke… a giant white Himalayan tiger!

But the chic and friendly criminology student only laughed.

"I suppose you'd like me to believe that white tiger is real," Cynthia said to her adversary. "But I'm betting it's a tulpa you created with the help of your old friend the Tea-Leaf Reader."

"Don't bet on it," Hal Overton said. "And even if he is a tulpa, don't forget, his teeth can still bite if the flesh is impure."

"We'll see about that!" the fashionably dressed detective said. "Here, kitty!"

To the surprise of Hal Overton—and dozens of mystified spectators—the white tiger trotted toward Cynthia and sat down at her feet. Cynthia reached down and tickled the formerly vicious beast under his chin. The big cat lay down and purred. Cynthia knelt down to pet it as it curled over onto its back, exposing its wide white belly for the private detective—and lonely orphan—to stroke.

"We'll see who's so smart next time!" Overton exclaimed.

"We sure will," Cynthia said. "After I perform a banishing ritual on this fella and send him back to the etheric realms!"

And that was the Case of the Tiger and the Tulpa. After a few days of rest, Cynthia went back to junior college and got back to work. But Cynthia was hardly prepared for the biggest case of her life—the very last case of them all!

It started on her very first day back at school.

Professor Gold pressed down on the remote control in his hand. The familiar *click-whirl-click* of the slide projector filled the dark lecture hall. On the wall appeared an image of a crime scene in a neat, modern, stylishly furnished home. On the plushily carpeted floor were the remains of a family of three—mother, father, and toddler son. Blood soaked the rose-beige deep-plush carpet. *DIE PIGS* was written on the wall in dried brown blood.

"Now," Professor Gold queried, "who can spot the clue in this picture?"

"Why, I know," John Collins blurted out. "It's the writing on the wall—that's the clue!"

Professor Gold nodded evenly. "That's true, John," he said. "That writing is a clue—and for the police, it's a pretty good one. But that's not the kind of clue I'm talking about. Does anyone see another clue in this picture—one that's a little more meaningful to them?"

The students shuffled their pens and papers, unsure of how to answer. Even Cynthia was stumped by this one. For once she hoped the professor wouldn't call on her!

"Cynthia," Professor Gold called out. "Why don't you give it a try?"

Inwardly Cynthia groaned. Gee, would she look like a fool. But if there was one thing Professor Gold had taught her, it was that looking foolish wasn't a very important thing in life. Not compared to finding the truth!

"I-I'm sorry," Cynthia stammered. "I don't know where to begin!"

"That's OK," Professor Gold said with a smile. "How about this: Look at the picture, and begin with anything that speaks to you—anything at all. It doesn't have to mean anything to anyone else but you."

Cynthia squinted and stared at the picture.

"Don't strain," Professor Gold said. "Relax. Let it come to you."

Cynthia was embarrassed at her faux pas—the

professor had gone over recognizing clues with her a thousand times!—but she quickly recovered. She let her eyes and face relax, just as the professor had taught her. She didn't so much look at the picture as sit with the picture, and let it tell her its secrets.

After a moment Cynthia stood up and walked up to the wall, becoming a part of the picture itself as the light shined bits of blood and bone on her neat yellow casual dress.

"This painting," she said, tapping on a simple painting of sunflowers on the wall of the gore-ridden home. "I know I've seen it before."

"Go on," Professor Gold said, encouraging his favorite student.

"It was at the City Museum. I went there when I was a girl. Mrs. McShane took me when I was sad. That picture—well, it cheered me up a little. I even bought a little postcard of it to take home, so I could look at it again."

"Keep going," Professor Gold said.

"Why, it's so cheerful it's almost as if—well, you would think someone in the family wasn't very happy, to need such cheering. And look at this," Cynthia said, moving toward the bookshelf projected on the wall. "Look at these books here—*Curing Melancholia* and *Be Happy*. Someone in this family was depressed!"

Professor Gold smiled, but Cynthia needed no more encouragement. She was on a roll!

"And that makes me think," Cynthia said, lost in the thrill of detective-time. "If you look at the angle of the gun and the blood-spatter patterns—"

Her jaw dropped open as she looked at the professor. They both grinned.

"I've solved it!" Cynthia said excitedly. "I've solved the mystery! The mother killed her husband and son, and then shot herself!"

Professor Gold smiled broadly. "That's absolutely right, Cynthia."

He turned toward the class. Cynthia returned to her seat.

"The clue is not the thing that tells you who committed the crime," he explained to the class. "The clue is the thing that tells you why *you* were called to solve this particular crime. The question is never *Who did it?* There's always one question, and one question only: *Who are you, and why are you here?*"

Professor Gold looked out toward the class, his green eyes bright and mischievous.

"Here's a question," he said. "How do you know who you are? Or to put it a different way: How do you know you're you?"

Cynthia furrowed her brow, confused.

"Why, I'm Cynthia Silverton," she said. "And I know because—why, because everyone says I am!"

"Now, Cynthia," Professor Gold said with a gentle smile. "You know *everyone* has often been wrong before. Remember when *everyone* told you there was no such thing as ghosts?"

"That's true," Cynthia said, puzzled. She rolled the professor's question over in her head, and over and over again, and slowly she felt the worst feeling come over her—like she was teetering on the edge of a cliff and had only just now looked down. She tried to shake off the feeling, but a little of it stuck behind, lingering in the corners.

"Now, what if I were to tell you," Professor Gold said, "that 'Cynthia Silverton' is nothing more than a clue to your real identity? Or rather, a set of clues?"

"A clue?!" Cynthia said. "Why, whatever could you mean?"

She had no idea what the professor was talking about, but now that she was on a case, she felt back on sure footing again. She'd never said no to a mystery before, and she wasn't about to start now!

Professor Gold looked at Cynthia seriously now, his smile gone.

"Now, Cynthia," he said. "I know you've faced many

mysteries before, and you're becoming an excellent detective—one of the best I've seen, to be honest."

Cynthia blushed and murmured an objection to the professor's compliment. But the professor caught her eye and held it.

"But this case," he said, "is like no other mystery you've solved before. In this mystery, you're both the client and the detective. You are the mystery, and the clues are both in you and in the world around you. You can't go back once you know the truth. You can never un-know what you know. Are you sure you want to tackle it?"

Cynthia pursed her lips and considered what the professor had told her. At first she felt scared by the professor's serious face and big words. Maybe some mysteries were best left alone. That was what people were always telling her, at least. Her boyfriend Dick sure seemed to think so, and Mrs. McShane would be happy if Cynthia never touched another mystery again! Maybe she was too young for this case. Maybe she should play it safe once in a while.

The long black road of a possible life curled out before her in her mind's eye—she would put mysteries aside, marry Dick, have children. They would join the club, maybe get a dog…

Or, this.

"I'm in," Cynthia Silverton told Professor Gold. "Let's solve a mystery!"

But Cynthia's joy was tempered by an odd, sad look in Professor Gold's eyes. It was almost as if he'd wanted her to say no.

Just what was this mystery, anyway?

"All right, then," the professor said. "Here's your case: Who are you?"

Cynthia started to laugh, thinking Professor Gold was joking. Of course Cynthia knew who she was! She was a teen detective, an orphan, and the best student at Rapid Falls Junior College. She lived with her beloved housekeeper, Mrs. McShane, and had passionate almost-sex with her fiancé, Dick, every Friday night.

But she looked at Professor Gold, and from the look on his face Cynthia could tell he wasn't joking at all.

"Who are you?" Professor Gold repeated. "Who are you when you aren't a college student? Who are you when you aren't Dick's girlfriend? Usually we define ourselves by the roles we play in life—daughter, wife, teacher. If we no longer have those roles, what's left?

"Who are you if you aren't pretty anymore? Who are you if you aren't so smart? Who are you when no one's looking? Who are you without the context you've built around yourself? Can those contexts—those connections—serve as a kind of armor to protect from the truth? And if that's the case, what might that truth be? That, Cynthia, is the mystery you have to solve. But you can still say no. Are you sure, Cynthia, you want to take on the case?"

Cynthia leaned forward in her chair. She felt a flutter of something dark and almost sickening in her stomach.

But underneath her fear, every part of Cynthia yearned for the truth. It was an urge that had been with her as long as consciousness, and maybe before. Like all urges, there was something a little unseemly about it, something embarrassing. But despite—or maybe because of—the ways it made her vulnerable, and sometimes weak, this urge was the strongest, most real thing she'd ever known. Maybe the only real thing at all.

Maybe, she thought, *that's who I am—I am a thing that solves mysteries, and is therefore useful.* But even as the words formed in her mind, she knew they weren't true enough for her lips. Surely she was more than just a tool to be useful! She had to be something more than that!

Then who was she?

"Yes," Cynthia said firmly to Professor Gold, even though the words were thick and frightening in her mouth. "I want to know."

Professor Gold gave her a look that was a little wry,

maybe even sad, and said, "I knew you would, Cynthia. Good luck. You might need it."

At home that afternoon, Cynthia's happy Irish housekeeper, cook, and surrogate parent, Mrs. McShane, fixed Cynthia her favorite fig-and-yogurt bowl for her afternoon snack. Cynthia sat at the kitchen table, listening to Mrs. McShane prattle on about the neighborhood gossip.

"Mrs. McShane," Cynthia said.

"Yes, dear?" the kindly, plump housekeeper replied.

"Who are you?" Cynthia asked.

Mrs. McShane laughed and looked at Cynthia funny.

"Now, dear girl," Mrs. McShane said, "you haven't been eating mushrooms from the woods again, have you?"

Cynthia laughed.

"No, not today," she said. She explained her new project to Mrs. McShane: Professor Gold wanted Cynthia to find out who she was.

"I guess I thought if I knew who you were," Cynthia said, "I could figure out who I am."

Mrs. McShane smiled at her beloved charge, but there was a little wistfulness around her eyes.

"But you already know everything about me you need to know," Mrs. McShane said. "I love you dearly,

I promised your ma I'd take care of you, and as long as I'm alive I will."

Tears came to Cynthia's eyes.

"I love you too," Cynthia said without hesitation. "But who are you when you're not with me? Who were you before I was born?"

"Ah," Mrs. McShane said with a wave of her hand. "That's a long story, and in my eyes, yer still too young to hear it. We got enough sadness in this house already. I like leaving mine outside the front door. Now, on to your other question: who are you?" Mrs. McShane said, a twinkle coming back into her eye. "Ah, that'll be quite an adventure for you, girl. You'll find out something the rest of us have tried to hide from you for many years now."

Cynthia felt her stomach drop and her vision start to blur.

"What's that?" she asked, fear creeping into her voice.

"That yer a grown woman, and ya don't need any of us anymore!" the housekeeper said with a vivacious laugh.

But that night, Cynthia couldn't sleep. She stood up in the middle of the night in her dark room and took off her white cotton nightgown and her white cotton panties and looked in the mirror. She was too thin, and the outlines of ribs pushed up against her chest. Her hip bones stuck out like corners.

Her many scars glowed in the dim moonlight. She felt like she was looking at a ghost.

Who was she? Who was this woman with this slim, pale body? With these scars from fights and falls and bad luck? With the small tattoo of the Unspeakable Symbol just above the neat, trimmed line of hair between her stomach and netherlands?

As she looked in the dark mirror, Cynthia had the strangest sensation. As if everything she was or had been could just float away—her body, her house, her mind, her beautiful and fashionable wardrobe—it could all just dissolve, and there would be no Cynthia left. Just some small pile of unloved-little-girl, some misplaced little abortion, a puddle of things no one wanted, left behind, a miscarriage not even worth cleaning up…

But almost as soon as the sensation hit her, she found it too ugly to bear. She shook it off by reminding herself about the people who loved her: her boyfriend, Dick; her teacher, Professor Gold; her lama; Mrs. McShane; and so many others. Rapid Falls had embraced Cynthia, and held her in its loving grasp, after the death of her parents.

She put her nightgown back on, as if to protect herself against fate, and went back to bed, telling herself, over and over, that she was real. And as long as she was loved, she could prove that she was real, and would never have to face her own terrifying nothingness again.

The next morning Cynthia overslept, and was late to Professor Gold's class for the first time. Cynthia flew into the classroom like a whirlwind, and all eyes were on her as she tried to take her seat without attracting any more attention.

Professor Gold looked at her sternly.

"Thank you for agreeing to join us today, Miss Silverton," he said dryly. "Perhaps next time you'll even grace us with your presence before class is halfway done."

Mortified, Cynthia stared at her desk and stammered out a response.

"I'm, I'm so sorry, Professor Gold. I was thinking about your question last night and—"

Professor Gold held up one hand to stop her. "It's OK, Miss Silverton. Just be on time tomorrow. Now, speaking of psychic attack, who can tell me how the Violet Flame meditation works?"

Cynthia shot her hand up, ready to answer. She was sure she knew this one.

"Give some of the other students a chance," Professor Gold said, an edge of irritation in his voice. "We all know your proficiency with the Violet Flame, Cynthia."

Cynthia blushed to her blond roots. Professor Gold called on Randy Grant instead.

Cynthia felt the same for the whole rest of the day—late and unappreciated everywhere she went! But that night she had an exciting event to look forward to: Cynthia's fiancé, Dick, was throwing a giant gala for his parents' twenty-fifth anniversary at the country club!

After school Cynthia had plenty of time to get ready, so she went for a walk downtown. Maybe Miss Elm, who owned the dress shop, would have something for Cynthia to wear tonight—a new blouse or a stylish piece of jewelry.

Cynthia was strolling to Miss Elm's, lost in thought, when she nearly tripped! Looking back to see what she'd stumbled on, Cynthia saw it was a long, skinny pair of woman's legs. Following the legs upward, Cynthia saw they were attached to the old lady who lived with her shopping bags in front of Hamburger Hank's.

Everyone just called the woman who lived in front of Hank's the Bag Lady. Looking at her now, Cynthia wondered how the Bag Lady came to be the Bag Lady.

Had she once had a different kind of life? Of course she had, Cynthia chastised herself. No one was born a Bag Lady. Cynthia had often spoken to the two town heroin addicts who hung around in Hank's, and now they waved at her through the window of the budget-minded hamburger restaurant. Cynthia waved back at Joanne and Yvette. Cynthia was as much a part of the scene at Hamburger Hank's as anyone—detective work made for interesting and unusual bedfellows!

But she'd never spoken to the Bag Lady. Looking at her now, Cynthia felt a funny little flip in her stomach, like she'd seen a secret she couldn't possibly understand yet—

Cynthia looked at the woman and tried to catch her eye. The Bag Lady ignored her.

"Hi," Cynthia said. "I'm—"

But just as she was introducing herself, she heard a commotion from around the corner and ran to the scene—just in time to see Hal Overton running out of the First Bank of Rapid Falls with a bag full of cash!

Without a second thought, Cynthia gave chase to the seasoned criminal. She thought she'd lost him when he made a swift left on Maple, but Cynthia knew the streets of Rapid Falls better than her own teeth, and she took the alleyways (and cut through Old Mr. Smithee's yard) to meet up with Hal Overton over by the slaughterhouse on Route 3.

Cynthia came out of the maze of alleyways just in time to see Overton heading into the slaughterhouse. Fuck. Cynthia's lungs burned, but there was no time to catch her breath as she followed Overton into the dank, foreboding warehouse.

The smell of blood and shit and the cries of animals hit Cynthia like a tidal wave when the door to the filthy slaughterhouse closed behind her. How often the lama had encouraged her to visit the charnel house to remind her of the brief sweetness of life—and now here she was!

But this was no time to meditate. With quiet stealth, Cynthia weaved through shit and cattle as she looked for Hal Overton. She caught him for a brief second by the pens, but lost him after one quick blow from his fist knocked her into a mess of blood and filth. In a moment she was back up on her feet and back on the chase.

She followed Overton outside, through a horrible labyrinth of caged animals screaming for freedom, and out to the docks beyond.

Stumbling with exhaustion and shock, mind numb and past fear, Cynthia finally had Hal Overton cornered—at the end of the longest pier in Rapid Falls.

The two nemeses stood at the edge of the pier as the sun went down over the Great Unfathomable Lake. Both the detective and the criminal, wet with sweat and blood, the smell of death and shit clinging to them, panted and looked at each other.

"Hal Overton," the charming young detective said, regaining her spunk. "I see that Sheriff Brown has let you out on a technicality again."

"Sure. And I hear you're on a big case, kid," the villain said, smirking with his horrible, swarthy lips.

Cynthia wondered how Hal Overton could have found out about her big new assignment. But she didn't dare ask, for fear of giving the criminal any advantage.

"No bigger than the dozens I've cracked before," Cynthia replied, perhaps a bit haughtily.

But a curious smile came over Hal's lips.

"Sure, kid," he said. "But don't forget, I owe you for getting me arrested again. And I've got my new ray gun to help me get revenge!"

Suddenly Hal reached into his pants pocket and pulled out what looked like a miniature machine gun with a curiously ovoid barrel.

Cynthia wasn't scared, though. She'd been training in Tibetan martial arts since she was a toddler! Thank Tara she wore her slacks today! With one swift kick she knocked the ray gun out of Hal Overton's spindly, spidery hands.

The villain lost his weapon but not his will, and he

threw a punch at the junior sleuth that connected with her left shoulder. Fighting back tears, Cynthia replied with a powerful jab, this one right to Hal Overton's windpipe. The cruel man lost his breath and fell to the ground, gasping for air. Finally, before Hal could recompose himself, Sheriff Brown came running over to help.

"Cynthia," Sheriff Brown said with an embarrassed look, vodka on his breath. "You saved the day again. I sure wish this guy didn't have such good lawyers."

Cynthia agreed. The legal system in Rapid Falls had a lot of technicalities, and Hal Overton and his team knew every one. But instead of joy, Cynthia felt a curious and unpleasant feeling as she watched the sheriff arrest the criminal. Like she was stuck in a movie, with the same silly scene playing over and over, until it became grotesque and lifeless.

Why, Cynthia thought, *it's almost like we're insects—all part of some kind of horrible, unconscious swarm!* Cynthia didn't like that thought at all. No wonder Professor Gold had warned her off this case!

Cynthia supervised Sheriff Brown to make sure Brown remembered to read Overton his rights and put him in the police car without injuring him. Then she went back to the police station to make sure the paperwork was properly filled out. Sheriff Brown was a bad alcoholic, which didn't help matters one bit. Ever since the Case of the Broken Wheel he just couldn't stop drinking, and Cynthia was pretty sure he'd stopped trying.

Cynthia was just checking the locks on the holding cells when she remembered—Dick's parents and their party at the country club! She was already late! Cynthia rushed to the country club without changing. Surely, she thought, it would be better to make an appearance, even not looking her best, than it would be to miss it altogether.

But as soon as she walked into the gala affair, Cynthia saw she'd horribly misjudged. Everyone else was wearing their best cocktail attire, some of the older folks were in formal wear, and everyone stared at Cynthia when she walked through the door in filthy dungarees.

Dick came rushing over to Cynthia before she even got to congratulate his parents, and pulled her right back out the door.

"What the heck?" the handsome young pre-med student said, eyes flashing. "How could you show up to my big night like this?"

"I'm so sorry!" Cynthia said. "Just let me explain!"

"I don't even know who you are anymore," Dick said, disgust curling the corners of his lips.

Cynthia felt tears spring to her eyes.

"But Dick," she said softly, "I thought you loved me for me."

Dick looked at her with revulsion on his face.

"I did," he said. "I loved the old Cynthia. The one who made such special fruit punch! Now you're like a different person. Showing up at my parents' big party in dungarees—and with a tooth missing!"

Cynthia poked around in her mouth with her tongue—he was right, of course. Sure enough, tooth number five, upper right, was gone and forgotten.

"I can explain," Cynthia rushed to explain. "I was fighting Hal Overton, and Sheriff Brown had been drinking again, and—"

Dick gave her another withering look. Cynthia felt like she was shrinking under his eyes. Just a few hours ago she'd felt so big and strong—now she felt like a speck of dirt.

"I think we need to admit this is over, Cynthia," Dick concluded. "If this is the best you can do—"

"I can do better," Cynthia whispered. But her words tasted pathetic to her as soon as they came out of her mouth, and she knew she would regret them for the rest of her life.

"And, Cynthia," Dick leaned in to whisper, as if to a child, as if she didn't know, as if it hadn't happened in the course of saving this town's sorry ass one more time, "you smell like shit."

Dick turned and walked back into the party. Cynthia fell to the cold, wet, sweet-smelling earth of the country club.

She felt like half of her had just been burned away.

I thought I'd always have Dick, Cynthia thought as tears fell from her eyes to the impeccably cut grass. First a feeling of rejection overcame her, then loss, then shame, and finally fear.

Without Dick, Cynthia thought again, *who am I?*

That night Cynthia went home alone. The house was dark and quiet. It was Mrs. McShane's night off and Cynthia had the house to herself. The junior detective was acutely aware of Mrs. McShane's absence. Cynthia wondered where the kindly housekeeper was.

It fell on her, as it sometimes did at unpleasant moments, that the person she was closest to on this earth was someone she paid.

The emptiness of the house felt frightening to Cynthia, and she was tempted to take one of the pills Dr. Summerisle had prescribed her for nights like this. If she took the pill she knew exactly how she would feel:

first tense, then hungry, then, after an odd and unhealthy snack, relaxed and drunkenly content. Then she'd fall asleep, probably within arm's reach of a bowl of ice cream and the TV, playing trashy crime dramas or romances.

But Cynthia wasn't so scared of being scared. Not yet. Life had not yet taught her just how fearful fear can be.

For now, Cynthia skipped her pill. Instead, without fixing her hair or even washing up, she took off her clothes and looked in her full-length mirror again, as she had the night before.

Her face was smeared with dirt, made worse by humiliating tearstains. Her eyes were red and puffy. When she forced a smile, she saw blood on her gums. A fresh set of bruises bloomed around her left breast, arm, and shoulder where Overton had attacked her.

A shiver went up Cynthia's spine as she realized how much she now looked like the Bag Lady. How easy it could be to end up living in front of Hamburger Hank's.

Even worse, she saw how little there was to anchor her to this world, and what a worthless world it was.

So who was she now?

Cynthia shook the question off, put on a clean nightgown, and went to bed.

The next day Cynthia sat desultorily through her school day, barely raising her hand once, even in Professor Gold's criminology class. She could tell she was annoying him. When she finally blurted out an answer to a simple question on forensics, Professor Gold practically bristled, and after class made an unkind remark—

"Cynthia, if I were you, I'd be working on my assignment rather than showing off my knowledge of Bullets 101."

Well, fuck you too, Cynthia thought about the attractive tenured professor. *Fuck you too, Professor Gold.*

After school Cynthia had her monthly appointment to speak with the lama about her spiritual training. As she drove up to the monastery in the high forest-draped mountains, she had to admit she was thinking less about how to dedicate her merit and more about all the personal problems she wanted to talk about with the illustrious and blessed master.

Cynthia had expected the lama to be sympathetic to her trials with Dick and Professor Gold. Instead, after she told him all about her horrible week, he seemed just as mad at her as Dick was.

"Too old," the lama growled, shaking his head. "I'm done playing with foolish children. No romantic problems. Go write Dear Suzy."

Cynthia's face fell. "I-I'm sorry," she stammered. "I know how valuable your time is—"

"And I have too little left of it," the lama said. "Go. If these are your serious problems in life, we're done."

Cynthia stared at him.

The lama stared back. And he didn't ask her to leave again.

Instead, he stood up, and left the room himself.

That night Cynthia understood fear a little more than she ever had before.

She didn't want to know it any better.

She took the pill.

She soon found herself in the familiar television/icecream haze. But instead of the slightly intoxicated contentment she was expecting, she felt lonely and confused. She tried eating more ice cream, but the stylish junior college student still felt like the witch in a fairy tale who shows up uninvited and ruins everyone's life.

Like everyone would be happy if she left, and no one would miss her if she were gone.

The next day Cynthia woke up determined to shake off

all this silly new negativity that had built up over the last few rotten days! She took a long, hot bath with Florida Water, styled her hair flawlessly, and made an appointment with the town dentist, Lou Frost, for a new tooth. She remembered to ask after Dr. Frost's disabled son and felt good when he told her the long story of trying to get little Herb in special education. She could tell he really needed a good listener, and she was happy she could be that listener for him.

One benefit of being an A-plus student was that Cynthia had rarely missed a day of school, and could afford to skip a day now. Instead of rushing to campus, she had a long, leisurely breakfast of Mrs. McShane's wonderful poached eggs, and insisted that Mrs. McShane join her for coffee and poppy-seed cake afterward. They had a nice chat and after breakfast Cynthia dressed in casual dungarees and a button-down blouse, topped it off with her mother's pearl amulet necklace, and went for a walk through town.

As she stopped at the bookstore to pick up some titles she'd ordered on astral projection, Cynthia was starting to feel like her old self again. So what if she didn't have Dick anymore? A man wasn't everything! And Professor Gold and the lama would come around, and if not, well, who needed them?!

I know who I am, Cynthia thought, confident and in her element at the bookstore, enmeshed in cultural signifiers and paperbacks. *I'm Cynthia Silverton, teen—* But she stopped herself. In a mere few months, she wouldn't be a teen, but a young lady of twenty.

She wouldn't be Cynthia Silverton, teen detective, anymore.

Cynthia shook off her temporary letdown and bought her books after chatting with the bookstore owner, Mrs. Washington, about advances in alien technology and the government's hidden programs of reverse engineering. But when she left the bookstore and stood in the hot sun, blinking, on the paper-thin edge of a good mood and abysmal sorrow, deciding what to do next, the Bag Lady across the street caught her eye again.

Again, Cynthia couldn't stop her bright and nimble mind from studying the older woman. Was the Bag Lady blond like Cynthia? Had she grown up in Rapid Falls? Had the Bag Lady once had a boyfriend like Dick? Had she, too, once been a junior college student?

With trepidation, Cynthia crossed the street and approached the older woman, nestled in her usual spot in front of the hamburger restaurant.

The Bag Lady didn't look up.

"Hi," Cynthia said. She crouched down to speak to

the woman at eye level.

The woman didn't answer Cynthia, and kept her eyes down.

"Can I grab you a burger?" Cynthia asked. "Maybe some fries?"

Now that she was close, Cynthia saw that the woman was indeed blond like her. But her face was so weathered and brown and wrinkled that she looked about a million years old. And yet, to Cynthia's surprise, she didn't look unhappy. If anything, there was something in the Bag Lady's eyes that almost made Cynthia forget her problems altogether—

But before the older woman could respond, or Cynthia could collect her thoughts, Cynthia heard a piercing scream!

"Sorry!" Cynthia called out to the lady, and ran toward the scream. It seemed to be coming from around the corner, toward First Street. Cynthia always felt good on a caper, and this time was no exception. Her blood was pumping and her lungs were full of oxygen as she ran. *I know who I am*, she thought again as she ran—

Then why do I keep telling myself that? she immediately thought next.

But her insight was cut short when she heard another scream, this one from even farther away!

Cynthia ran down to Third Street, didn't see any-thing, and kept running. But she couldn't find the source of the scream. She looked down alleys and side streets and poked into doorways, but found nothing unusual.

Finally she stopped running and stood in the middle of the block, panting.

She looked around. No one was around.

No one was around at all.

"Shit," said the teen detective. "This is not fucking good."

Cynthia felt Hal Overton before she saw him—felt his aura as he pulled up beside her in his late-model Creamsicle-orange Cadillac.

Everything seemed to slow down and speed up at the same time as Cynthia turned and started to run back to town. But before she got twenty feet she heard the bang of a pistol and a bullet sparked the concrete next to her spotless tennis shoes.

She stopped running.

Overton came up behind Cynthia and pushed his .357 Magnum into her back.

"Look who's the fucking clever one now," he said.

That was the last thing Cynthia remembered before Overton held his handkerchief, soaked in chloroform, over her nose and—

♣

There was a green field. It seemed to go on forever; Cynthia was sure she could see the curve of the earth at the edge of it. And at the end of the field were Cynthia's mother and father. They were alive! Oh, she'd always known it. Always known that they wouldn't leave her like that. They reached out to her, and Cynthia's heart overflowed—

"Wake up, you meddling little cunt."

Hal Overton's uncouth words woke Cynthia from her blissful chloroform high.

She sat up and looked around.

They weren't in a lush green field, as Cynthia had dreamed. Instead, they were out in a wide expanse of dry green-brown scrub surrounded by woods thick with pine and live oak. Cynthia made a quick calculation based on the sun, the moss, and the plants around her—and saw that they were in the middle of nowhere! They were miles and miles away from a city, a town, electricity, or running water. Cynthia knew this area—it was one of the least-developed spots in the country, and due to the thick woods, one of the hardest to search.

She was stuck.

Cynthia and Hal Overton looked at each other as

Cynthia stood up. Cynthia bit her lip nervously. She'd been in plenty of jams before, but this was the worst!

"It's finally curtains for you, you meddling teen detective," Hal Overton said with a grin. "Now strip."

Cynthia took off her clothes as slowly as she could. When she was naked, the criminal grinned. Cynthia felt his eyes take in her cold and goose-fleshed hips, her bruised thighs, lingering on the tattoo on her lower abdomen.

"And now hand over that expensive jewelry your parents left you," he said with pleasure.

"No," Cynthia said, through tears. She'd given up on solving her case, or winning her battle with Overton. But this was too much. She felt something twist inside of her. She was drowning, drowning from the inside out, and it was like nothing she'd ever felt before: naked, with nothing to protect her.

"Not the pearl amulet Mother left me," Cynthia said quietly. "It's all I have left of her. I promise, promise on her grave, I'll deactivate its sphere of protection! I'll do it right now! But please. Let me keep the pearl. Mother wore it every day, and it's all I have of her."

Overton laughed cruelly and pointed his gun at her. "Hand it over."

Crying, Cynthia unclasped the pearl necklace and threw it at Overton's feet.

"Keep going," he growled.

As tears fell from her eyes Cynthia took off her gold earrings, the lapis bracelet Professor Gold had given her, and the engagement ring from Dick she still wore. She tossed them all at Overton's feet.

But as awful as it was, and as frightened as she was, there was some part of Cynthia that felt lighter with each item she tossed over.

Cynthia had always excelled. Always won. But underneath it all, she now saw, there had always been an undercurrent of fear. Fear of failure, fear of exposure—and worse, fear of her own darker self rising up and taking over. Now she saw how much that fear had stained her consciousness, cut into her potential for joy.

Well. There was nothing to be scared of anymore.

Overton laughed at Cynthia.

"Good luck finding your way home, kid." And then Hal Overton gave Cynthia a funny kind of look—as if he knew something she didn't. "And solving that big case."

Overton jumped into his car, and sped away.

Cynthia looked around, horrified. She was entirely alone.

Naked, Cynthia stumbled toward the forest, crying and

cursing her fate. Soon her feet and legs were cut and bleeding, and then her hands and forearms. She was filthy.

What had she done to deserve this? How did she end up here? She did everything right and somehow she still ended up in this accursed place, alone not just in body but in spirit.

She was entirely alone in the world. She knew no one would find her here.

No one but Mrs. McShane would miss her. No one, it seemed, was willing to do the job of loving Cynthia for free.

She shivered from the cold.

After the first two days she was too miserable to feel hunger, but her body shook from lack of food.

There was nowhere to go. Cynthia knew her science—naked and starving and dehydrated, she could easily die from exposure before anyone found her. She was at least a hundred miles away from a paved road.

After three days she knew she wasn't going in any direction that made sense.

She wondered if death would come soon.

"So this is how it ends," Cynthia said to herself. "After all my adventures fighting crime, my great dates, my perfect outfits, and my 4.0 average at the junior college. I thought I was so special, and now look—turns out I'm just another victim of the evil Hal Overton. Just another dead girl in the woods!"

But as horrible as it was, there was something freeing about the thought. Never again would she struggle to impress the lama or Professor Gold. In death she would never have to worry about letting anyone down again. And at least she would die keeping her secrets and her shame—no one would ever know about the times she went too far with Dick, about the shortcuts she took on the Case of the Golden Dawn, about all the bad and ugly thoughts she'd had about everyone in Rapid Falls. Maybe it really was better to die young and leave a spotless corpse!

And then, just as everything was starting to fade to red and black around the edges, just as the ground was starting to feel indistinguishable from the air, a miracle happened: She found a stream of clear running water. She drank on all fours, like a dog. Water had never tasted so good. Nothing had ever been so wet.

She hadn't eaten anything since Overton had abandoned her. After gorging herself on water, she rested by the stream for a little bit. Her blood was thinned and her mind was cooled, and she could think a little more clearly.

After she drank a little more water, she remembered the obvious. Fish live in water, and this water was clean and running strong.

Cynthia doubted her ability to catch fish with her hands. But there were plenty of bushes and trees around, and it was easy enough to fashion a kind of spear out of a long twig.

She watched the cold water, squatting on the bank of the stream. She failed on her first try, and her second, and her twentieth, and her thirtieth.

But on her thirty-second try, she caught a fish. Once it was caught, she didn't know what to do with it. It flapped around on the stick, iridescent scales glimmering wet, trying to live.

Cynthia decided she would live instead.

She set the fish on the shore and let it die, and then she used the sharpened stick to widen the gash she'd made in it and held it in the water, hoping the blood would flow out. Some did. When it was as clean as she could make it, she scraped off the scales, picked off some of the skin, and ate it raw.

At first it was hard to swallow. She'd lost her taste for food, and her mouth puckered up at the first bite. But after a few bites her mouth began to water and her stomach growled and she ate most of the small fish at once.

Maybe, she thought, *I will not die today.*

With that thought the world around her took on a quality she'd never seen before—a kind of sharp reality that she knew must have always been there, but she'd never perceived before.

Had green always been so beautiful? Had water always tasted so good?

So this is my life! she thought. *This is life now!*

Cynthia ate fish for three days, then found a blackberry bush nearby and ate what the birds had left. After a few more days she trusted herself enough to recognize dandelions and purslane to eat. She had no books, but she had years of study and her own intuition. A few times over the next few weeks she made herself sick eating the wrong plants, but each time she recovered.

Cynthia had always taken her esoteric upbringing for granted before, but now she saw how truly lucky she'd been. She knew so much, she now saw—the doctrine of signatures, plant communication, the phases of the moon.

She missed her parents.

Every day was a miracle.

From far away she heard animals—maybe wolves, maybe coyotes, maybe feral dogs. But she never saw them. She did spend time with birds of all kinds, though, who seemed not to know enough to be scared of her. She knew it was ridiculous and arbitrary, but she could only bring herself to kill the fish for food, never the birds. *How ridiculous life is,* she thought, *that you have to kill in order to live!*

At first she tossed her fish bones back in the stream. Then one day she noticed a hawk, just a few feet away from her, picking at the head. She'd never seen a hawk so close before. She was so lonely she ached, and had to hold herself back from embracing him. From then on, she always left the scraps and bones from her fish out on the riverbank, and the hawk visited more often. Cynthia came to think of the hawk as her friend, and worried about him when he wasn't around.

At first, the silence in the woods terrified her. It bore down on her, made her throat burn from pressure. She tried talking to herself, but that made her feel like reality was slipping away, like she was moving into a tilted, confused world. When she wanted to use her voice she chanted or sang instead, and that made her feel sane.

Soon the silence came to be a comfort and a friend.

Days passed, then weeks. Cynthia thought that once she got her strength back, she would look for a road out again. But as the weeks passed, a road out started to seem like the plan of a silly child. She knew she was unlikely to find a road at all. And if she did, where would she go? What difference would it make? Professor Gold had once pointed out to her that all of life was a kind of locked-room mystery—after all, we were all stuck here in this life together, with no good way out. She would be in her locked room wherever she went. There was no big mystery in walking across a room. This was as good a place to enjoy the room as any.

The days got shorter, and colder. Cynthia couldn't figure out how to make any clothes, but she did make a kind of blanket for herself out of moss and dried leaves. As the days got colder still, she began to worry. But then something incredible happened. She'd gotten in the habit of going on long walks every day, to look for food and moss and just to walk. And then there it was, like an answer to her prayers: a dead coyote, not too badly mauled, coat almost intact. It took weeks to skin it and clean it, but Cynthia had a very warm, dry fur to wear through the winter.

In spring Cynthia made I Ching sticks from wild yarrow stalks in the special method Professor Gold had taught her. When she threw them she got hexagram 186: the lotus in the mud.

Image: Lotus seeds can only be planted in the mud. Filth and pain are superior foods.

Meaning: All life must come to an end, but your day is not today. Tomorrow isn't looking so good either. You have one precious human life, and you're stuck with this one: Use it wisely, and try not to fuck it up.

At first Cynthia missed her old life in the city. But as time went on, she thought about it less and less. And as her hair turned gray and she felt her breasts sag and her face grow soft, she came to appreciate her life in the woods more and more. Here she had everything she needed. Here she was really alive in a way she'd never been around other people. Here each moment was real in a way she'd never known was possible.

More and more when she looked back on her old life in Rapid Falls, her life with fancy clothes and a big house and restaurants and hospitals, she felt like she was thinking about someone else. Some overwound girl who worried all the time about things that didn't matter at all. And while she loved that girl, she also felt a little sorry for her. Too busy with her mysteries and meditations and bills and dates to see that life was passing her by before she even knew what she was missing.

Cynthia thought about all the locked-room mysteries she'd solved over the years as a teen detective. But life as herself, inhabiting her own body and mind, which had seemed so mysterious and elusive, was nothing but another locked room. There was no way in or out. Even if you could escape, you'd be in another locked room: this fucked-up world, which you could get out of easily enough, but never get back into once you left.

But this locked room was all that she had—all anyone ever had, or ever would. Everything you could look for, it was here, in this room—in these woods, in this life. There was nothing else. Here we all were, Cynthia figured, locked each in our room, in this house together, and the best we could come up with was ways to murder each other.

But you could find everything you wanted in the locked room, if you looked hard enough. The most interesting things weren't right there on the surface. They hid in the corners, under the carpet, behind the potted plants. Always getting a little farther until you stopped looking. And then somehow, mysteriously, if you proved to the interesting things that you would really listen, that you would really see them, they would come to you.

The less space you carved out for yourself in this room we shared, she now saw, the more space you left for everything else—things that were so much more interesting and important than she could ever have dreamed. And a coyote skin and a fish bone could tell you everything you needed to know, if you listened when they spoke.

Maybe, here in the woods, she'd found a way out of the locked room, she thought sometimes. Or maybe she'd just really, for the first time ever, found a way in.

One day Cynthia went back to her camp after collecting dandelions and found an envelope on her favorite rock. Across the front was written, in crooked familiar handwriting:

Cynthia

Cynthia opened the envelope. It was thick paper, maybe silk—how much she had forgotten over the years!—with a string-and-tie seal. Inside was a plain card. Written on the card was:

Cynthia,

A+.

Mystery solved.

P.S. I miss you. I love you. You are my friend.

Sincerely, Professor Gold

THE END

THE MYSTERY AT KILLINGTON MANOR

OR

THE FEELING OF SEEING CLEAR BLUE SKY AFTER BEING LOST IN THE WOODS

THE KILLINGTON FAMILY

Mrs. Killington, also known as Mrs. Kitty, also known as Livinia Killington, also known as Liv: Matriarch of the Killington family.

Poppy Killington-Wade: The youngest Killington. Great-granddaughter of Mrs. Killington. Daughter of Maisie Killington-Wade.

Maisie Killington-Wade: Poppy's mother. Mrs. Killington's granddaughter.

Daisy Killington-Marr: Maisie's twin sister. Also Mrs. Killington's granddaughter, and Poppy's aunt.

Josh Killington-Wade: Husband of Maisie, father of Poppy.

Jacob Killington-Marr: Daisy's husband. Poppy's uncle.

Aunt Julia: Distant relation to the Killingtons.

THE STAFF OF KILLINGTON MANOR

Charlotte Henderson: Cook.

Katherine Schwartz: Maid.

Thomas White: Groundskeeper.

Henry Kowalski: Gardener.

Johnny Deen: Driver.

Olivia Smith: Hunter.

CHAPTER ONE

Poppy Killington-Wade, sixteen years old, lay in her bed in Killington Manor reading *Mycology at Home: A Beginner's Romp Through the Friendly World of Fungus.*

It was close to midnight, September 24, 1949, a Saturday night. Killington Manor, in the countryside of New England, was quiet. This weekend, like most weekends, there were guests at the house, all now asleep. Poppy's parents did not like to be alone. Poppy's mind wandered from mushrooms to one of the guests. Something about the guest was fascinating to Poppy, but she couldn't place her finger on what, exactly, fascinated her.

The fascinating guest made Poppy think of a dream she'd had a few times. In the dream, Poppy was in a town or city she knew from her everyday life—Boston or Providence or nearby Rapid Falls, usually—when she saw a corner, and realized she'd never turned that way before. In the dream she would turn down the street and find a whole new city, one more delightful and lively than the one she knew in real life. In the dream-city there were bright colors, interesting shops, unusual people of all kinds, and restaurants filled with strange and wonderful foods. *I can't believe I didn't know it was here,* she would think in the dream. *How didn't I see it?*

Sometimes after this dream Poppy would wake up in the middle of the night and walk around Killington Manor, smoking cigarettes she nicked from the box her mother kept on the coffee table. She would walk as far as the edge of the woods, but never go farther—the woods at night scared her, and she could never bring herself to step in after dark. Now, in her muddled, late-night thoughts, she imagined the fascinating guest standing in the woods at night, perfectly safe, comfortable and at home in the dark.

Just when Poppy thought she was on the verge of an answer to the question of what was so fascinating about the guest, she heard something that made her freeze: footsteps in the hall.

Poppy quickly turned off her light and lay perfectly still. She wasn't supposed to be reading so late.

The footsteps kept going, and by the time the footsteps passed, Poppy was ready for sleep. She left the lights off and as she felt sleep take over, she tried to remember what it was she had been about to understand about the fascinating guest. But she didn't remember. Or, maybe, had never understood at all.

CHAPTER TWO

Earlier that day, on Saturday afternoon, Poppy had come downstairs to wait for the guests in her usual weekend outfit of a blouse and a skirt and saddle shoes. Maisie wore a black dress with a nipped waist and a wide skirt, black high heels, a few strings of pearls, and a large ruby cocktail ring. She looked at Poppy's outfit and frowned.

Poppy was the only child of Maisie and Josh Killington-Wade. They all lived at Killington Manor with Maisie's twin sister, Daisy, and Daisy's husband, Jacob— they were the Killington-Marrs, and had no children.

"You're not a child, Pop," Maisie had said, frowning at Poppy. "Please do go and put a dress on. And some real shoes."

Maisie always knew the right thing to wear. Poppy knew she should consider herself lucky to have a mother who knew such things—what to wear, what to read, how to hold a drink just so. But *luck* was never what came to mind.

Poppy went back to her room. But instead of changing, she lay on her bed and read a book about the tall redwoods in California. Some of them lived for thousands of years. She tried to picture a tree a thousand years old, and three hundred feet tall, with bright red wood. She took a break from reading midafternoon to watch a blue jay fly by her window and land on a maple tree at the edge of the woods. Soon Maisie would pick a pine tree from the woods for Christmas and Thomas, the groundskeeper, would enlist some friends from town to come and help him cut it down. A few months after that Thomas would tap the maple trees for syrup, and would let Poppy help check the taps once or twice. Thomas was from Ireland and always wore a hat.

Dinner would be served at eight. At seven, Poppy put on a pink dress and high heels and came back downstairs. The guests had arrived and it was cocktail hour in the great hall, the biggest room in Killington Manor, with high ceilings that ate up nearly half the house. It was where Maisie and Daisy kept their record player and, last year, had had a wet bar installed along the wall nearest the kitchen. The stairs from the second floor led into the great hall on the right; on the left was the dining room, and then the kitchen. Maisie prided herself on her decorating, and had recently had the great hall redone in bright velvet sofas and chairs.

The little party was in full swing. First Poppy said hello to Martin Guerro and Peter Gaines, close friends and roommates for fifteen years, regulars at Killington Manor. Martin was from Buenos Aires, Argentina, and Peter was from Newport, Rhode Island. Poppy knew they had an apartment in New York, but they seemed to spend their lives traveling from weekend to weekend, country house to country house.

Martin looked at Poppy with a sharp, kind eye. "Look at what a young lady you are," he said. "No more toys for you."

They're not smart, Poppy thought. *But they're sweet.*

Maisie came over to their little group, looked Poppy up and down, and gave a quick nod of approval at her dress. After Maisie's nod, seeing her sister was pleased, Daisy followed her sister, and joined them with an anxious little smile. Daisy and Maisie were twins, but not identical, and everyone—most of all Daisy and Maisie—seemed to know who was the better sister. Maisie had inherited the famous Killington beauty, while Daisy was, they said, *perfectly fine*. Maisie had a will of iron, controlling everything that went on at Killington Manor, from the choice of china patterns to who Josh's friends would be. Daisy seemed to have no will at all, other than to make her sister happy. While Maisie moved with sharpness and determination, nearly always in a crisp and perfect dress, Daisy moved softly and aimlessly, with great effort and too much thought.

Poppy stood around until Maisie and Daisy forgot about her, howling with laughter at a funny story told by

Martin and Peter, and then snuck off to the sofa by the fireplace, where her favorite of the guests sat: Mrs. Kitty, Poppy's great-grandmother, and Mrs. Kitty's best friend, Aunt Julia.

Mrs. Kitty's real name was Livinia Killington. Maisie and Daisy had always called her *Grandmother*, stiffly. No one remembered when Poppy had given her a nickname. No one who knew Liv Killington before Poppy came along would imagine anyone calling her Mrs. Kitty. But her great-granddaughter brought out a warmth in Mrs. Kitty that her children and grandchildren had failed to find.

Poppy sat next to Mrs. Kitty on the green velvet sofa. Mrs. Kitty was, and always had been, the oldest person Poppy knew. She was a big woman, and seemed to grow every year, not just in size but in number of petticoats and pieces of jewelry and hats and hair. There was always more of her. Mrs. Kitty could be intimidating, and her hardest face could stop anyone in their tracks. But she never had a shred of hardness for Poppy. Instead, she put a warm arm around Poppy and pulled her close. She smelled like tea rose.

"They've got you dressed up like a doll," Mrs. Kitty said. "Tomorrow you can put your dungarees on and get back to your garden." Poppy smiled. "My rough-and-tumble girl."

Even though Poppy only saw her great-grandmother a few times a year, Mrs. Kitty always knew Poppy in a way that no one else did—or, she would learn as life wore on, few others would. When they were both younger, Mrs. Kitty would bring Poppy souvenirs from her travels around the world: candy-covered almonds from Italy, a little onyx statue from Mexico, a music box from France. But Mrs. Kitty didn't travel anymore, although she sometimes brought Poppy petit fours from a bakery in Boston.

"Tell me, Poppy," Mrs. Kitty asked, "was the mushroom picking good this year?"

Poppy had to admit that, since the last time they saw each other, her mushroom hunting skills had barely improved. Being able to pick her own mushrooms had been a goal of Poppy's for a few years now, but she could still hardly tell an *amanita* from a *bolete*, or a true chanterelle from a false.

"Well, we'll just have to go to Siberia," Mrs. Kitty said. "The shamans will set you straight—straighter than any book ever could. It's been on my list of things to do for many years. You must meet them before you're too set in your ways."

Poppy knew that they wouldn't really go to Siberia, but they began making plans nonetheless: boats, trains, Siberian guides, special mushrooms that made you see things that weren't exactly there.

"We must go in late summer," Mrs. Kitty said. "And Mr. Yakut is absolutely the best guide, although, like all of us, he's getting on in years. But no one knows the forests like Mr. Yakut. We'll see if he thinks you're ready for an initiation. I think yes, but you don't argue with the shaman. I'll write him forthwith when I get home. And we still haven't been to Rome—you're the perfect age to see it for the first time. And then of course we must go to London, too."

They made imaginary plans until Mrs. Kitty grew drowsy.

"I need to close my eyes for just a moment before dinner, my love," Mrs. Kitty said after they'd plotted out a tour of experimental theater in Rome. In ten seconds she was snoring.

While Mrs. Kitty dozed, Poppy turned to the last guest at Killington Manor: Aunt Julia, who sat on the blue armchair by Mrs. Kitty. Aunt Julia was somewhere between sixty and one hundred, and she wasn't exactly anyone's aunt—she and Mrs. Killington were third or fourth cousins—but everyone in Killington Manor knew her as Aunt Julia. She and Liv—or Livinia or Mrs. Kitty or Mrs. Killington—had been friends since they were girls at boarding school. Aunt Julia also lived in

Boston, and once or twice a year she joined Mrs. Kitty for a weekend in the country at Killington Manor. Maisie and Daisy tolerated her presence with admirable, determined restraint.

Aunt Julia took a big sip of her cocktail, which was bright green and nearly glowed. "Good for the nerves," she said. "Now, little Miss Poppy, what were you reading in your room all afternoon?"

Poppy smiled again, and wondered how Aunt Julia knew she'd been reading. Aunt Julia was the fascinating guest Poppy would think about that night when she went to bed. Unlike Mrs. Kitty, Aunt Julia seemed to shrink every year, flesh diminishing, white hair drawn in an ever-tighter bun, dresses growing slimmer and plainer. She reminded Poppy of a sparrow, tilting her head and always listening. Poppy told Aunt Julia about the redwoods.

"Oh, the redwoods are extraordinary," Aunt Julia said, to Poppy's delight. "I was in California back in the teens—many more trees then, I'm sorry to say. Each one a world unto itself. A great spiritual presence. My dear friend Louis had a little art colony up in the woods— nudists and surrealists! All gone now, sadly."

Poppy didn't know what any of that meant, but before she could ask, it was time for dinner. Dinner was roast beef and creamed spinach, and Poppy was hungry and ate seconds—and would have had thirds, if not for a sharp look from Maisie.

In the middle of dinner, a shot rang out from the woods. Everyone froze.

Maisie rolled her eyes. "It's the gamekeeper," she said. "I mean, game-girl. The hunter."

"Game-girl?" Peter said.

"Well, we haven't had a proper staff since before the war," Maisie said. "And no gamekeeper since then. The groundsman shot a few quail for us but was never good with deer. So we brought in a man from town to take a few deer for us every year. You know Daisy and Jacob love venison."

"I do!" Daisy said, excited to be acknowledged. "I love venison!"

Maisie went on as if her sister hadn't spoken: "Josh does not. Too gamey. I could take it or leave it, but it seems to me if they're on our property, we ought to eat them. And then this year the man didn't show up, and a girl shows up here with a gun, and says the man is gone and she's his daughter and she'll be shooting our deer this year. A girl! But she's got one buck already. She's been butchering it in the kitchen. Utterly revolting. We gave her a room for the season by the laundry—

I was keeping my quilts in there. You know, I'm not a bad shot myself."

Poppy noticed Mrs. Kitty and Aunt Julia exchange a look. She'd noticed they often exchanged a look when Maisie talked. The look was a kind of amused shock, Poppy thought, but there was another element in it, one she couldn't name. She'd heard people describe her mother as *bold*. Maybe that was what the look was about: Maisie's *boldness*.

Another shot went off. Poppy had seen the girl hunter in the woods earlier in the week. The hunter stood so still, pointing her gun at something Poppy couldn't see, that she startled Poppy when she moved. Poppy, scared, ran away.

"Anyway," Maisie said. "Did you hear? The Cranes just bought a place in New York. They can hardly afford it, but we have one, so I guess they thought they'd try to keep up."

"She never does anything original," Daisy said. "*Never.*"

"Oh! And Binnie Tyler is going to Egypt with that new friend of hers. Of course, she's paying for the whole thing."

There were a few more shots but no one commented on them, and the adults kept talking, and then dinner was done and they drifted back out to the great hall to keep drinking and keep talking. Poppy went to bed, and read her book about mushrooms, and heard footsteps. She woke up the next morning, convinced herself her mother surely couldn't expect her to dress for breakfast, even with guests in the house, put on a simple blouse and skirt and her saddle shoes again, and went downstairs to find out that Mrs. Kitty was dead.

CHAPTER THREE

All the adults were already in the great hall, looking tired and glum. Aunt Julia sat on the pink sofa with tears running down her face. The staff stood in a row, as if lining up for inspection. Poppy noticed the hunter standing with them, even though she wasn't really staff.

Poppy stood in the entrance to the room, looking around in confusion. She realized she'd forgotten to brush her hair, which was long and thick and blond in the summer and light brown in the winter. She began combing it through with her fingers.

He father came over and stood awkwardly in front of her.

"Pop. I have very tragic news. Your great-grandmother is gone," Josh said to Poppy, his voice syrupy. "We lost her last night."

Poppy's face fell. At first she thought she'd misheard her father. Then she looked at the grim faces around the room and realized she'd heard correctly.

Mrs. Kitty was gone, gone forever, and would never put a warm arm around her again. Poppy thought, *Now no one knows me. Now no one in this house knows me at all.* She felt herself start to shiver, and wrapped her arms around herself. *For the rest of my life I will be a stranger, here and everywhere, because the only person who knew me is gone.*

"Lost?" Aunt Julia said. "You didn't misplace her, Josh. She died."

Poppy sat close to Aunt Julia on the pink sofa. She started to cry, but she knew better than to sob in front of her mother, and so she bit her lip until it hurt to make herself stop. Poppy saw that Aunt Julia noticed this, and frowned.

You don't understand, Poppy thought. *I am a ghost and I have no home.*

"Grandmother didn't wake up at her usual early hour," Josh explained to Poppy. "After coffee, your mother went to check on her. But unfortunately, we were too late."

Jacob, sitting nearby, reached out to take Aunt Julia's hand.

"I know you must be overwrought," he said. "But you have our greatest sympathies."

Aunt Julia opened her mouth to speak, then thought twice and shut it. But she did swat Jacob's hand away.

"These things happen," Josh said. "We are gifted with life, but not eternal life. Now God has called her home."

Poppy looked at her father. He looked, as he often did—as he was—like a stranger. His face looked like a movie star's: handsome and controlled and entirely fake. He kept the sad look on for another moment or two, maybe even a second too long, and then raised his eyebrows and let the sad look drop.

Soon a man from the funeral parlor came. His hair was slicked back and he had a complicated mustache. He talked to Maisie and Daisy for a while and then two men came in behind him, carrying something like a cot.

It's like she was never here, Poppy thought. *It's like she was a drawing on paper, and they're just erasing her away.*

Poppy's hands started to shake. She felt like she was dissolving, slipping into nothing. *They'll erase me too*, Poppy thought. *They'll rip up my garden. They'll make me wear dresses and shoes that hurt, and no one will stop them. I will be a stranger forever, and no one will ever know me again…*

But then Aunt Julia stood up.

"If no one minds," she said, "I'd like to say goodbye."

Maisie's face grew tight. "Of course, Aunt Julia. This must be very sad for you."

The adults went back to the funeral director, talking about money and funeral plans and money again.

"Of course we want it to be a beautiful ceremony," Maisie said. "With no expense spared. But I can't imagine we'll need—I mean, it'll just be us, really. No need to go too far."

Aunt Julia turned to Poppy and took her hand.

"Come with me, dear," Aunt Julia said. "I know it's frightening. But I think it'll be better if you say goodbye."

CHAPTER FOUR

Mrs. Kitty's room was Mrs. Kitty's room, even though she hadn't lived at Killington Manor for forty years. Mrs. Kitty had first married at eighteen, to the Marquis de Lyon. The Marquis lived only a few days after his shark bite off the coast of Cuba, just two years after the wedding. Next was Ronnie Jones, with his ranch in Wyoming—the marriage didn't last long, but it produced the woman who produced Daisy and Maisie, and Mrs. Killington kept half the ranch. Then there was a banker from New York, and an oil man from Texas, and a painter in Madrid. Even though she'd only visited Killington Manor two or three times a year since she'd left, and generously allowed the twins to use it as their own, she'd insisted that no one touch her room.

Poppy was struck by how everything in Mrs. Kitty's room seemed dead now. When she was alive, it had always been the brightest room in the house. The dresser was littered with knickknacks and perfume bottles, photographs and paintings lined the walls, and stacks of books covered the floor. Poppy imagined the room empty, its soft rose walls painted white, and all of Mrs. Kitty's treasures in the trash heap, alone and abandoned.

She'll clean it out as soon as she can, Poppy thought. *She'll paint away every trace of her.*

Lying in bed was Mrs. Kitty. Poppy couldn't quite believe what she was seeing. This body was definitely her, but also not her at all. In death she was pale and gray, with shades of blue around her mouth.

Like a baby, Poppy thought. *Like a kitten, helpless and alone.*

Aunt Julia went to Mrs. Kitty, and touched her face and kissed her softly on the forehead. "Goodbye, dear friend," she said. "I'll see you soon enough."

Poppy held Mrs. Kitty's hand. It was cold and stiff.

"I love you, Mrs. Kitty," she said, and suddenly great big sobs came out of her mouth. Her mother would be angry if she heard, but Poppy couldn't stop. Aunt Julia put her arm around her, pulling Poppy into her shoulder.

"Take something to remember her by," Aunt Julia said, when Poppy's sobs quieted. "She was yours far more than she was theirs."

Poppy took a little white ceramic cat she'd always liked from the dresser, and the book Mrs. Kitty had been reading, *Murder Comes to Cape Cod*. When they left Mrs. Kitty's room, the man with the mustache and his workers were just coming in to take Mrs. Kitty away.

Aunt Julia went back to bed to rest for a while. Poppy

wanted to go to her garden, but didn't want to cause any trouble, not today. Instead, she went to her room, changed into a dress and high heels that she knew her mother would like, and went downstairs. But the adults were gone.

Poppy stood in the middle of the great hall, doing nothing, feeling oddly scared in her loneliness. She'd lived in this house all her life, but now it seemed eerie and empty.

I am a stranger here, she thought. *I am entirely alone.*

Suddenly, the hunter came out from the dining room. The hunter wore a white apron with bloodstains, some old and brown, some fresh and red. She was a woman of twenty- or thirty-something who almost never spoke. No one at the house, staff or guests, had seen her smile. Poppy remembered the hunter's father, a tall, thin Black man who, like his daughter, almost never spoke, at least not around Poppy.

"Cook asked me to let you know lunch was ready," the hunter said. "Guess the rest of them went out on the horses."

Poppy was embarrassed to be caught so confused and alone, and didn't say anything. The hunter went back into the kitchen. Poppy walked alone into the dining room, where the table was set for nine. All the plates were empty except Poppy's, which held a slab of roast beef from last night and a scoop of mashed potatoes. She sat at the table and ate lunch alone. It was so quiet in the house that she could hear the servants in the kitchen, talking as they ate their own lunch.

After a minute, Poppy realized they were talking about her.

"Poor thing," Cook said. "Her grandmother dies and no one says a word to her."

"Great-grandmother. But you can't feel too bad for her," the chauffeur said. "She'll get all this one day."

"Nah," the maid said. "They'll spend every last dime. Lucky she's pretty, she can marry up."

"What's *up* from a Killington?"

Poppy started to feel hot. How dare they talk about her? And who were they to pity her?

"I don't care what happens to any of them," the maid said. "They don't care about us. When my mother passed, I got half a day off for the funeral—and they docked my pay."

"I don't think they care about each other much more," the gardener said. "Going riding and visiting, today. And leaving the kid here! A girl needs parents."

Poppy felt so angry and strange she couldn't take it for another second. She thought, *They will not, they cannot.* How dare they think she needed anything at all. *They* needed, they needed everything and she needed nothing—she would fire them all, send them right out into the cold.

She stood up and walked to the kitchen to tell them all off, anger and shame so strong, Poppy felt like her feelings were tumbling out of her, leaving a trail of broken glass behind her. But just as she reached the kitchen door, it opened, and the hunter came out.

They almost knocked into each other. Poppy stepped back.

"Thought you might like some fresh bread with your lunch," the hunter said. She held a ceramic dish with hot sliced bread in it.

Poppy felt ridiculous and angry and sad all at the same time. She started to cry.

The hunter put the bread down on the table and said nothing.

"I'm sorry," Poppy said. She felt, somehow, that the hunter knew the cruel words she had almost said, words she was already ashamed of.

"That's OK, miss," the hunter said. "Losing someone you love is a sad day. But losing someone who loves you, that's a sadder day."

Suddenly the horror of the situation fell on Poppy

all over again—Mrs. Kitty would never speak again, or laugh, or eat a petit four. The whole of the future would be without her, and she without it.

Poppy cried fresh tears, overwhelmed.

"What should I do?" Poppy said to the hunter.

"Eat some bread," the hunter said. "And then go change into real clothes, and go for a long walk in the woods. And when you come home, you'll be tired, and you can go right to bed, and you won't have to see any of them again for the rest of the day."

Poppy felt embarrassed again, and grabbed the bread off the table and ran away.

CHAPTER FIVE

Poppy did what the hunter said—she ate the bread alone in her room, and then went for a long walk in the woods, where she looked for mushrooms and followed a hawk for a while, missed dinner, and did feel a little bit better when she got home. The adults were in the great hall drinking and listening to records again. *It's like they're celebrating,* Poppy thought. *Like it's just another weekend, and no one died.* Poppy snuck past them and went to her room.

In her bedroom, in her boyish pajamas that Maisie hated, Poppy lay in bed until she heard the last adult go to their room. She held her book about redwoods but didn't read it. Near midnight she turned off the lights and tried to sleep, but sleep was far away. She lay in bed, then sat up and turned on the lights, then turned them off again. Instead of sleeping, Poppy thought about Mrs. Kitty, so cold and still, and all the things she'd heard the servants say about her. And about how every time she went mushroom hunting, for the rest of her life, there would be no one to tell about it, because no one would care.

Finally Poppy sat up and turned the light on again. She was further from sleep than ever. She carefully opened her door and peeked both ways down the hall. The coast was clear, as they said in the movies. Poppy especially liked the Thin Man movies, which she'd seen at the movie theater in town when they showed old films on Sundays. Maybe someday she could have a life like that, drinking martinis and spending her days with a handsome man who took care of her money and loved her, just as she was—although, of course, she would have to be as pretty and slender and witty as Nora for that to happen. And a dog—Poppy had been so taken by *The Thin Man* that she'd begged her parents for a dog so she could name it Asta, but they didn't like dogs, or movies, or Poppy, and said no.

Poppy was skilled at leaving her room at night with no one noticing. She crept her way down to the great hall, across the cold floor to the dining room, and to the wide door to the kitchen—but at the door, she stopped.

Someone was talking inside. Two people, in fact. Poppy closed her eyes and listened very hard. The two voices, after a moment, worked themselves out as Aunt Julia and the hunter.

"May well be," Poppy heard the hunter say. "People've killed for less, that's for sure."

"Murder knows no reason," Aunt Julia said. "Except its own."

"True," the hunter said. "A crime has its own logic, and that's half the battle of solving it."

"I sometimes think of a murder as a kind of poem," Aunt Julia said. "One that calls for interpretation, both literary and psychological. And little Miss Poppy, you can come join us in the kitchen. There's one piece of pecan pie left, and we've made some tea."

Poppy was mortified. But her curiosity—that thing that made her wander the grounds of Killington Manor at night, that made her read books about trees and mushrooms, that made her eavesdrop when fascinating people were in the house—overwhelmed her embarrassment.

Poppy opened the door and stepped in. Aunt Julia and the hunter were sitting at the big kitchen table, where the servants worked and ate their meals, with plates of pie crumbs and full cups of tea in front of them.

"Miss," the hunter said in acknowledgment.

"Come and sit down," Aunt Julia said. "We're talking about mysteries."

Poppy sat down next to Aunt Julia. When Aunt Julia lifted her teacup, Poppy noticed the strong smell of alcohol coming from it.

"For grief," Aunt Julia said, tipping her cup.

Poppy got herself the last piece of pie, on a pretty white plate with pink roses on it, and ate it ravenously as they talked.

"Olivia here," Aunt Julia said, gesturing to the

hunter, "until six months ago, was a police officer with the Boston Police Department. And a very good one. If I recall correctly, she cracked the case of the Chinatown strangler."

Poppy was astonished. Somehow she'd never thought of what the help did when they weren't at Killington Manor. The game-girl was Olivia? And she'd been a police officer? Her mind raced.

"We all worked very hard on the case," Olivia said modestly. "The whole gang chipped in."

Olivia had a funny kind of an accent, Poppy noticed, almost British. Poppy's favorite teacher at school was an amateur linguist, and after he met a new person he could tell where they were from in five words, or very often just one. But Poppy couldn't tell where Olivia was from.

"Oh no," Aunt Julia said. "That isn't true at all. You solved the case, my dear, you and that doctor you found in Boston."

Olivia held back a smile. "Thank you," she said simply.

"Olivia here," Aunt Julia went on, "was asked to leave the force after a, well, I think it was a misunderstanding, wasn't it?"

Now Olivia started to laugh. Aunt Julia laughed along with her. Poppy wasn't sure what they were laughing at. What kind of misunderstanding could be so funny?

"That's one way of putting it," Olivia said, choking back laughter.

"Well," Aunt Julia said, "I've been blessed by many misunderstandings myself, with many a gentleman. And a few gentlewomen, too."

This set off a new round of laughter from Olivia and Aunt Julia.

"Now," Aunt Julia said, "I can only hope to meet a gentleperson interested in misunderstandings with a lady of advanced age."

No, Poppy thought. *They can't mean that?*

"You know," Aunt Julia said to Poppy, "your Mrs. Kitty had quite a life. Did you know she wrote books?"

"I didn't!" Poppy said. "What kind of books?"

How did I get to be sixteen, Poppy wondered, *and know so little?*

"Murder mysteries," Aunt Julia said. "She published her first in 1921, then five more after that. They were very popular, but she lost her taste for writing—it does happen."

"Did you write books too?" Poppy said to Aunt Julia.

Aunt Julia smiled. "No," she said. "I've been entertaining the idea of writing a memoir. But time is brief, and I'd rather spend it living than writing."

"I hope you do, though," Olivia said. "Your aunt is a bit famous."

"No, no," Aunt Julia said modestly. "I've been helpful a few times."

"Ha!" Olivia said, with good humor. "Julia damn near single-handedly solved the murder of the Turkish ambassador in London. And the kidnapping of the Red Canary in Paris. She's well known to all us coppers, and it's an honor to meet her."

"You solve murders?" Poppy asked. "Like—" She stopped herself from saying *like Nick and Nora*, thinking she would sound childish.

"Hardly," Aunt Julia said, but from the way she said it, Poppy knew it was true. "But I enjoy being helpful where I can."

"And that case in the North End last year," Olivia went on. "And the very troubled situation in Maine."

"Well, I don't like to be bored," Aunt Julia said. "Boredom is the great enemy, you know," she said to Poppy.

"I think so too!" Poppy said. "It's terrible! How long were you with the police?" she asked Olivia.

"Nine years on the force," Olivia said. She frowned.

"She was a rare good one," Aunt Julia said.

"So what—" Poppy wanted to ask why Olivia wasn't with the police anymore, but she blushed when she remembered the misunderstandings. "I mean," she started again. "When did you stop working with them?"

"About six months back," Olivia said.

"Not everyone is so broad-minded," Aunt Julia said to Poppy, "about certain proclivities. And authorities do not like those who resist corruption."

Poppy had no idea what that meant, but she nodded as if she did. She was terrified of this moment ending—of saying or doing the thing that would cause Olivia and Aunt Julia to realize Poppy shouldn't be here. Sometimes Poppy would sit with Maisie and Daisy when they talked—half-understood words about money and other women and husbands—and when they realized Poppy was listening, they would shoo her away.

"So how did you become a hunter?" Poppy asked. "If you don't mind my asking, of course."

"I do not," Olivia said. "I was kicked off the force, my pop was a gamekeeper and a hunter, I've always been a good shot, and, well." She shrugged.

"Come now," Aunt Julia said. "That's enough for one night. Time to get some sleep. We'll start again in the morning."

Poppy stood up and left to go back to her room. Behind her she heard Julia and Olivia cleaning up the kitchen, and realized she should have helped.

Start what? she wondered.

Back in her bed, Poppy still couldn't sleep. Again she

tossed and turned. Once, during another weekend party a few years ago—her mother and aunt, the husbands, another crowd of friends—they'd all decided to go for a walk in the woods. All the adults were talking about other adults they knew, who they married and how much money they had, or hadn't. Poppy lingered a little, dragging behind. The woods themselves were much more interesting than the adults: She saw mushrooms, their names half remembered from a mycophilic nanny, and trees she'd learned the names of from a little girl's guide book she had when she was a child—birch, maple, oak. She got so absorbed in the woods that when she looked up, she couldn't find the adults at all. She was alone.

Poppy was scared. She'd disliked the adults' company, but she knew they would protect her. She'd been alone in the woods before, but she always stayed close to home. Now she was lost and alone.

Don't be a baby, she told herself—but for some reason that thought made her even more scared, and she felt like she might cry. But Poppy made herself be strong. She remembered to look at the sun to direct her, but she was so turned around, and the woods so thick, she couldn't tell east from west. *I will not cry*, Poppy told herself. *Under no circumstances will I cry.*

She got more and more frightened, and was sure

she was walking in circles. The underbrush scratched her ankles, and the bushes raked her forearms, and her shoes were heavy with mud. And just when she'd worked herself into a shameful mess, she saw it—a clear long expanse of blue sky. She kept walking and suddenly she was out of the woods, on the top of a hill, and the long blue sky and the cool empty beach and the vast gray ocean were all there, right in front of her, spilling down the hill. She didn't know where the adults were, and she didn't care—all she needed to know was that they hadn't seen her when she was scared. All was right with the world.

But Poppy felt, somehow, like a different person than she was before she got lost in the woods. And after that day she decided to learn how to pick mushrooms and learn the name of every single thing in the woods—a project she was, admittedly, still working on.

That was almost how she felt after talking to Olivia and Aunt Julia in the kitchen—the feeling of seeing clear blue sky after being lost in the woods.

She wanted to feel it again.

CHAPTER SIX

Monday morning Poppy got dressed in old dungarees and a worn blouse and, carefully avoiding the dining room, where the adults were having breakfast, snuck out the back door and ran to her garden behind the house. The fresh smell of green plants and dirt immediately made her feel better. The basil was drooping, nearly done for the year, but the rosemary looked strong. She quickly watered everything, pulled a few weeds, and ran back to her room to dress properly for the day before her mother knew what she'd been up to.

Poppy was happy to see when she came downstairs that breakfast was over and she wouldn't have to eat with the adults. She was hungry, though, and went into the kitchen to see what she could find. Olivia and Aunt Julia were drinking coffee at the big kitchen table where the staff worked and ate their meals. Poppy was immediately jealous that they'd met for breakfast without her.

"Morning," Olivia said.

"Good morning, dear Poppy," Aunt Julia said. "Charlotte, would you mind making me a poached egg? I slept right through breakfast. And Miss Poppy might like a few as well."

Poppy wondered for a moment who Charlotte was,

but she noticed Cook nod in return. So Cook was named Charlotte! Poppy wondered how she'd never known the cook's name before. It seemed to her to open a door to something, knowing Cook's name was Charlotte.

Charlotte went to work making eggs. While they ate, Aunt Julia asked Poppy all kinds of questions. What did she study in school? What were her plans after? What did she do with her free time?

"Well," Poppy said. "I suppose I'll get married after school." No one had ever asked her questions like this before, and her face felt hot and strange.

Aunt Julia nodded, but Poppy got the impression her answers disappointed Aunt Julia.

"But what do you enjoy?" Aunt Julia asked. "You're such a smart girl. You must have interests."

"I—" Poppy began, but she stopped herself. She wanted to say that she loved her garden, but that was not a good topic, and her throat grew tight, and they finished their breakfast in silence.

"Those were excellent eggs, Charlotte," Aunt Julia said. Charlotte nodded in agreement. "I would ask for your secrets but I know better than to think you'd tell me."

"Yes," Poppy chimed in. "Very excellent, thank you."

Now Aunt Julia and Charlotte exchanged a look, like Aunt Julia had exchanged with Mrs. Kitty when Maisie talked about venison. Poppy felt stupid, and wondered what she'd done wrong. But Aunt Julia turned to her with a sharp and open face and Poppy felt that whatever it was, she'd been forgiven.

"Now," Aunt Julia said. "Olivia and Poppy, I was hoping you might accompany me to Liv's room."

"Do you need something?" Poppy said.

"Yes," Aunt Julia said. "I need to find out who murdered my friend."

CHAPTER SEVEN

Poppy thought she must have misheard, but followed Aunt Julia and Olivia up the stairs. Something told her that whatever they were doing, wherever they did it, she wanted to stay with them as long as they'd let her.

Mrs. Kitty's room, in her death, now felt haunted and eerie. Poppy, Olivia, and Aunt Julia stood in the middle of the room. Olivia and Aunt Julia began sifting through Mrs. Kitty's things.

"What are you looking for?" Poppy asked.

"Clues," Olivia said.

"How will you know if something's a clue?" Poppy asked.

Olivia shrugged.

"I have a friend in Paris," Aunt Julia said, "who's working on a definitive answer to that. But for now, just use your judgment."

Aunt Julia saw something on the vanity and picked it up. Poppy got excited and thought maybe it was a clue, but when she got closer, she saw that there were tears in Aunt Julia's eyes. She was holding a necklace. Even Poppy, who didn't care about jewelry, could tell it was a cheap fake, with a big red piece of glass where a real gem might have been.

"Is it a clue?" Poppy said.

"To who killed her?" Aunt Julia said. "No. A clue to sixty years of friendship. We bought this on our first trip to the seashore together. We were girls then. We went to Miss Bradford's School, where they tried to turn us into ladies. Thank God they failed."

"But you *are* a lady," Poppy said. "Of course you are!"

Aunt Julia let out a laugh and wiped her tears away and put the necklace in her pocket.

"You say that to me again," she said, "and we'll never speak again."

Olivia and Aunt Julia both laughed. But before Poppy could figure out what was so funny, Olivia, to Poppy's great surprise, crouched down, got on all fours, crawled under the bed, and came out with something in her hand.

Poppy and Aunt Julia looked at her. Olivia was holding a teacup. Poppy recognized it—it was from one of the everyday sets of china kept in the pantry.

"Ah," Aunt Julia said. "So that's how they did it."

"Did what?" Poppy asked.

"Poisoned her," Aunt Julia said.

CHAPTER EIGHT

Aunt Julia led Olivia and Poppy across the bright green lawn to the garage, which was down the hill, by the entrance to Killington Manor. Aunt Julia took a small pipe out of her pocket, along with a box of matches, lit the pipe, and began to smoke it. It smelled different from the tobacco Poppy's father sometimes smoked.

"For arthritis," Aunt Julia explained. "Very beneficial."

"Where are we going?" Poppy asked. She could hardly keep up with Aunt Julia and Olivia.

"Into town," Aunt Julia said. "We have work to do. Questions to ask."

"Should I get the chauffeur?" Poppy asked.

Aunt Julia laughed. "We need privacy and efficiency, two things a chauffeur can only hinder. Besides, driving is great fun. No one's taught you how?"

"No," Poppy said. "I didn't—I mean—well, someone always drives me."

"Ah," Aunt Julia said. "You will learn, my dear, that relying on others is not the path to happiness. This is the great error of the rich."

"Amen to that," Olivia said. "Some of them aren't much better than children."

"Very true," Aunt Julia said as they reached the garage.

"Poppy, you really must learn to drive for yourself."

"And cook," Olivia said. "Nothing like being able to make yourself a decent meal. And hunt, of course. Kill the food yourself, all the better."

"I can garden," Poppy said with excitement, forgetting that she wasn't supposed to talk about it. "My cabbages last year were as good as Cook's! I think she used them at Christmas dinner."

Poppy saw Aunt Julia and Olivia trade a small smile at her excitement. It wasn't a mean smile, but Poppy felt the anxious feeling from last night—that she would do something wrong and Olivia and Aunt Julia would send her away. She cursed herself—always ruining a good moment with her garden!

Please don't send me back to them, please don't, I can't, I can't, I will not—

"Then you're off to a fantastic start," Aunt Julia said. Poppy breathed a sigh of relief. She promised herself she'd try to be less stupid going forward.

Aunt Julia and Olivia got in the front of Aunt Julia's Studebaker, Poppy got in the back, and Aunt Julia drove them off the grounds and into town.

"Do you really think someone killed Mrs. Kitty?" Poppy asked.

"I know someone killed her," Aunt Julia said. "Did

you notice, when we observed the body, the blue tinge around her lips? Clear sign of cyanide, by an inexperienced poisoner."

"But that's impossible," Poppy said. "We would have heard if someone came in the house to do that. And wouldn't they have stolen something?"

Olivia and Aunt Julia traded another look. Poppy realized what that look meant.

No one had broken into the house to kill Mrs. Kitty. Someone already in the house was the murderer.

It can't be, Poppy thought. It was impossible.

"But some of the staff have been with us since before I was born," Poppy said. "They—"

But she stopped herself when she realized: They didn't mean one of the staff. They thought another Killington, or a friend, had killed Mrs. Kitty.

It couldn't be true. But Poppy didn't dare say that to Aunt Julia.

"Olivia," Aunt Julia said. "Do you think you might have any friends left at the coroner's office?"

Olivia smiled.

"I do," she said.

The coroner's office was on the edge of town. They drove by the police station, with a dirty look from Olivia, and then to a plain brick building at the end of Old Police Road.

"Pull 'round," Olivia said. "Not sure who's at the front door, but Gregor'll let us in the back."

Aunt Julia drove around to the back of the plain brick building and stopped by the back door. Olivia got out of the car and knocked. A man with black hair and a funny face opened the door. He smiled broadly to see Olivia, and Olivia smiled too. They shook hands and talked for a minute before Olivia waved Aunt Julia and Poppy over. They got out of the car and joined Olivia at the door.

"Miss Julia, Miss Poppy, this is Gregor Koscavitch, assistant coroner."

"Miss Julia," Gregor said, with an accent Poppy couldn't place. The accent made Poppy a little anxious. Her parents had always told her to watch out for foreigners. But she trusted Aunt Julia, and Aunt Julia trusted Olivia, and Olivia trusted Gregor, so, Poppy reasoned, Gregor must be all right.

"It's a pleasure to meet you," Gregor said to Aunt Julia. "A great pleasure. You're well known in Poland from the Case of the Murdered Seamstress. They still talk about that one in Krakow. And of course, all of Europe knows of the theft of the Nairobi Diamond. We all cheered when you proved that girl's innocence."

"Oh, I hardly had anything to do with it," Aunt Julia said. Then she turned somber for a moment and looked at Gregor. "Were you able to bring your family with you to the States, I hope?"

"No," Gregor said plainly, "I was not," and suddenly no one was smiling anymore. Olivia looked at the ground. Poppy knew there had been a war in Europe, which was why they couldn't get good help, or the best fabrics, or sometimes even tomatoes anymore, and she guessed this conversation had something to do with that, although she didn't know what. Aunt Julia put a hand on Gregor's shoulder, and said nothing.

"But come in," Gregor said, forcing himself to brighten up. "I hear you have a teacup for me to look at?"

"Yes indeed," Aunt Julia said, and Gregor led them all inside the building.

The smell in the coroner's building was horrible— meat and chemicals all mixed up into something even uglier than each alone. They walked down a hallway past six closed doors until they reached an open one. Poppy was a little scared to enter, thinking it might be full of dead bodies—but it was just an office, with white walls and plain wooden chairs and a messy desk, piled high with papers and books. They all went inside and sat down.

From her handbag, Aunt Julia pulled out the teacup Olivia had found under Mrs. Kitty's bed, which she'd carefully wrapped in brown paper. She handed it over to Gregor.

"Now," she said. "What can you tell us about this?"

Gregor looked at the teacup and immediately began to talk.

"Porcelain drinking cup, relatively recent origin, with faint residue of what appears to be tea in the bottom quadrant." He sniffed the cup. "No obvious odor," Gregor said. "And no unusual appearance."

"We have reason to believe," Aunt Julia explained, "this cup was used in a poisoning."

"Very well," Gregor said, barely blinking an eye. "We have tests for that, and tests we shall do."

Olivia and Aunt Julia and Poppy all thanked Gregor and stood up to leave. But before they did, Aunt Julia turned back to Gregor and put a hand on his shoulder one more time. Gregor looked at Aunt Julia and didn't smile, but he put his hand over hers for a long moment before they left.

Their next stop was the bank. Aunt Julia explained to Poppy that there might be an important clue in finding out who had the most to gain from Mrs. Kitty's death. Aunt Julia drove them to the old stone bank building, the very heart of town, and, once inside, went right past the tellers and the desks and the small offices to the office of the bank president. In front of his office was the prettiest woman Poppy had ever seen sitting at a desk, typing on a typewriter that made loud and satisfying noises. She seemed very happy to see Aunt Julia.

"Miss Julia!" the pretty woman said.

"So good to see you, Bess," Aunt Julia said. "How are the children?"

"Wonderful, thank you," Bess said. "And my sister is so much better—we can't thank you enough for convincing Dr. Brown to see her. Now, what can I do for you?"

"We don't have an appointment," Aunt Julia said. "But do you think Mr. Collins might have a moment for us?"

"I'm sure he will," Bess said. She went into the office behind her, closed the door, and then came right back out to show them in.

The office looked to Poppy like her father's study—a room of leather and dark wood and paintings of horses where nothing interesting ever happened. Her father often sat alone in his study at night, drinking and listening to classical records and sometimes reading books about money and war. The bank president, Mr. Collins, was flabby and soft and harried-looking. He, too, seemed happy to see Aunt Julia, and stood up to shake her hand.

"Julia," he said. "Always a delight. Should Bess get you coffee? Or tea? Please, all of you, sit."

Aunt Julia, Poppy, and Olivia sat down and declined coffee and tea with thanks. Mr. Collins offered condolences for the late Mrs. Killington and then asked what he could do for them. Poppy noticed that Aunt Julia was different when she talked to Mr. Collins—sweeter and, maybe, dumber. She introduced Poppy and Olivia—saying Olivia was one of Poppy's tutors—to Mr. Collins, and then began.

"Now," Aunt Julia said. "You know how confused I get with all these accounts and numbers and everything! But I'm trying to instill a little sense in my dear great-grand-niece here—I don't want her to end up an old fool like me. So I'm hoping we could go over a few things."

Aunt Julia asked a lot of questions and Mr. Collins answered them all. Poppy understood little of it. It was all about accounts and inheritances, taxes and probate.

"If I may," Olivia said. "For the purposes of helping Miss Poppy learn her arithmetic and, as Miss Julia says, a bit about handling her money—you said Mrs. Killington 'took care of her.' Could you tell her what she's inherited?"

"Well, most of it," Mr. Collins said. "I have to say, it came as a surprise to her mother. I was not aware that they were not aware."

Poppy didn't understand, but she noticed Aunt Julia and Olivia grow very sharp.

"I'm sorry," Olivia said to Mr. Collins. "Do you mean…?"

"Oh, apologies, apologies," Mr. Collins said. "I thought you knew. The late Mrs. Killington changed her will just about a year ago. The bulk of it is to be held in a trust for Miss Killington-Wade here until she comes of age. Her parents got a…well, a generous sum. A very generous sum. They're provided for. But I do think it was not as they hoped. The bulk of it will go to the young Miss Killington-Wade."

"Oh," Olivia said.

"Oh," Aunt Julia said. Poppy saw that they both seemed blown over by this, but she didn't understand why. She always had plenty of money and had never thought about where it came from, or why she seemed to have so much of it.

Mr. Collins looked at her. "I'm sorry, I thought your parents would have explained this to you—do you understand?"

"I don't know," Poppy said.

"What he's saying," Olivia said, "is that everything that was your great-grandma's is going to be yours. She was a very wealthy woman, and now most all of that will go to you, when you're of age."

Slowly, this sank in to Poppy. All of it? Hers? *But*

I'm just a child, she almost said, but then she realized that would be uncouth, and besides, wasn't true. She was almost a lady. Or a woman, or an adult, or whatever she would be that wasn't a child. If Aunt Julia wasn't a lady, Poppy was sure she didn't want to be one anymore, either.

Is this real? Poppy thought. *Can this be real?*

"And the house?" she asked. "That's mine?"

"That will be yours as well," Mr. Collins said.

"And that includes the grounds?" Poppy asked. "And the gardens?"

"Yes," Mr. Collins said. "All of Killington Manor will be yours. The house, the grounds, the woods, and everything in it, except your parents' personal effects. But everything that falls under the estate will be yours— the house, the grounds, the outbuildings, the woods, all belongings that were in the house."

My garden, Poppy thought. *My mint. The maple trees. Mrs. Kitty's books. All mine.*

"And may I ask," Aunt Julia said, "who's in charge of the trust?"

"Her parents, of course," Mr. Collins said.

"Oh," Aunt Julia and Olivia said again, but it was a different *oh*—one with some dismay attached.

Poppy felt her heart sink a little. *They will take it all,* she thought. *They will rip out the maple trees and clean out Mrs. Kitty's room.*

"And if she wanted," Olivia asked, "could she have someone else in charge of the trust? Someone more, um, frugal?"

Poppy's heart rose again, and she looked at Olivia with gratitude. She felt like an arrow had pierced her heart and unlocked a stream of hope so bright it almost hurt. Was it really possible? A real life?

"Well!" Mr. Collins said. "You'd need a lawyer for that. But I'm here to help, and to fulfill our clients' wishes. We wish all our clients at the Bank of New England a pleasant banking experience. We pride ourselves on it! But I can't make that change myself. The Killingtons have always used Berry, Hale, and Barrington. They've been your family's lawyers for three generations now. I'm sure they'd be eager to help."

Everyone looked at Poppy. She realized she ought to say something.

"So they work for my parents?" Poppy said. "These lawyers?"

"Of course," Mr. Collins said. "And very aggressively, I might add."

"Then I think I will need my own lawyer," Poppy said. She thought, *This is the most grown-up moment of my entire life.*

They all thanked Mr. Collins and hands were shaken all around and Poppy and Olivia and Aunt Julia left.

On the street outside, autumn was starting to blow in. Poppy wrapped her jacket around her tightly. She felt dizzy. So much had changed so quickly. The world was entirely different than it had been just a few hours before.

Mine, she thought. *My cabbages, my mint.* She imagined building a greenhouse, an ornate old-fashioned conservatory with white trim and glass all around. *Orchids*, she thought. *Oranges and limes. Mrs. Kitty gave it all to me. She knew me. Someone knew me and I am not a stranger, not here in my own life. She saw me and knew me and left me everything, because I am real. Now she is gone but she knew me, and loved me, and planned all this for me, for me, only for me.*

They all got back in the car. "And now," Aunt Julia said, "we'll go see about a new lawyer for Poppy."

CHAPTER NINE

Aunt Julia took them to a small brick office building a few blocks away, in downtown Rapid Falls. A doorman let them in. Like nearly everyone they'd met today, the doorman, Roger, was excited to see Aunt Julia. Aunt Julia asked about Roger's wife, who Aunt Julia had apparently helped in a dispute with her boss at a dress factory.

"You really came through," the doorman said to Aunt Julia, pumping her hand up and down. "You're a rare bird, you, keepin' your word. A rare bird!"

They took the elevator up to the fifth floor, where Aunt Julia led them into the strangest place Poppy had ever seen. It was like something from the future. All the furniture was modern and streamlined like something from a movie, chrome and leather in irregular shapes. But they brushed past the waiting room and into an office where they met a young man who Aunt Julia introduced as Carl Marlbur, and everyone sat down to talk.

Marlbur was young and Poppy thought he was the handsomest man she'd ever seen. She couldn't take her eyes off him. Aunt Julia gave him a brief summary of the situation.

"Well, the court would have to approve it," Mr. Marlbur said. "But they're usually amenable to this kind of change. Is there a problem in the family? Profligate spending? Something like that?"

"Yes," Poppy said, who suddenly realized, again, that she should be talking. All her life she'd talked too much, and now not enough! How would she get it right?

"Pro—profligate spending," she went on. "If I let them control it, I'll never see any of it. They'll—" She was going to say, *They'll take my garden, they'll pull up my carrots and throw them away*, but she stopped herself. "There won't be anything left," she continued.

"And who would you like to be your new trustees?" Mr. Marlbur asked.

Aunt Julia stood up and looked at Olivia. "Perhaps we should give Miss Poppy her privacy."

Olivia started to stand too, but Poppy stopped her. Everyone sat back down.

"Don't," she said. She turned back to her new lawyer. "Aunt Julia. I'd like her to watch my money for me. Mrs. Kit—Mrs. Killington trusted her, and so do I. I want her in charge of my money." She looked at Aunt Julia. "If that's all right with you, of course," she said.

"If it will make you happy," Aunt Julia said, with a small smile. "And perhaps Mr. Marlbur would be a good addition as well—someone who has experience with these things, and is likely to be around longer."

"Yes," Poppy said, feeling very grown up again. "Would that be all right, Mr. Marlbur?"

He smiled. Poppy thought he was even handsomer when he smiled. "Yes. And I would be careful to set it up so you could remove either of us, at any time. And the court would weigh in, of course, on the decisions we made together. But all in good time. I assume you're all right for money now?"

"I am," Poppy said. "I mean, I think so."

She imagined drinking martinis with Mr. Marlbur, like Nick and Nora. And they would give a martini to Asta, too.

"Well, this could be easy or it could be hard," Mr. Marlbur said. "First I'll talk to your parents' lawyers. Ideally, we'll all settle this like gentlemen, as they say. That means we get together and work it out. If not, we can go to court. For now, I can go to a judge this week and he can make sure your parents don't reallocate the assets in the meantime." To Poppy's blank look, he said, "So they don't move the money around, or try to hide it. It could take a few weeks or it could drag out much longer."

"And the house," Poppy said. "I need to keep the house, and the grounds."

"They certainly wouldn't be able to sell the house, if that's what you mean," Marlbur said. "Or make any serious alterations to the property. Even if they were to try, we would get a judge to halt it."

Poppy smiled. *Judges*, she thought. *I have lawyers and judges on my side, and Mr. Marlbur and Asta.*

They made their thank-yous and goodbyes and walked out and back down to the car. Poppy took one long last look at Mr. Marlbur on the way out. She could practically see the martini in his hand.

In the car, Aunt Julia declared it was time for lunch. She asked Olivia if she knew a spot where they could go together; Olivia suggested a Chinese café she knew where all were welcome. They drove to the south side of town.

Poppy had known that the south side of town existed, but she had never crossed River Street before. When she went into town she always kept to the north side, where the shops her mother and aunt liked lined the streets. Her mother had always told her not to cross River Street, because of the people who lived there—Poppy knew the words her mother used weren't nice, but she also didn't doubt that the south side of Rapid Falls was a dangerous place to be.

Now she looked out the window with curiosity. There were small, neat houses that gave way to brick apartment buildings that gave way to a busy shopping strip. Poppy was shocked to see people everywhere, all different kinds, shopping and talking and walking and arguing, selling clothes and fruit and snacks from stands and pushcarts, everyone just living their lives, right out in public. On the north side of town, of course people walked outside and said hello to friends, but everything else was behind closed doors—no one would dream of exchanging money right out on the street, or letting their children play on the sidewalk.

Poppy was amazed. It was just like her dream, where she found a part of town she'd never been to before. Here it was, in real life, and it wasn't scary at all. No one looked like a robber or a thief or a kidnapper—everyone looked perfectly nice, as far as Poppy could tell, and no one was doing anything bad at all.

The restaurant was a café of exactly the sort Poppy had never been in before. It was busy and loud and everyone, everywhere, was talking. And everyone seemed to know Olivia, who now talked up a storm. She was smiling and introducing Poppy and Aunt Julia to half the café—Vinnie and Mick and Georgia and Louis—as they walked to their table. Poppy had never imagined that Olivia knew so many people, from all over. And they all seemed to know her, and like her. Suddenly an ugly thought came to Poppy's mind— Olivia had never talked much at Killington Manor because Olivia didn't like the Killingtons.

They sat at an uneven table with rickety chairs. A Chinese man named Bennie, who Olivia also knew, dropped menus on their table and gave them small hot cups of tea.

Poppy looked at the menu and didn't see a single word she recognized, except *rice*.

"How about if I order for us?" Olivia said. "Been here about a hundred times, I ought to know what's good."

"But do get the *char siu*," Aunt Julia said. "I haven't had any since Taiwan." Aunt Julia took a small silver flask out of her handbag and splashed something from it into her tea before she drank it. "For exhaustion," she said, drinking the tea in two big gulps.

Bennie came back and Olivia ordered for them. Olivia asked Aunt Julia about the Mystery in Brooklyn Heights and Aunt Julia told a fantastic story about a murder and the missing earring that led her to find the killer. Then she told a story about a missing heiress in Hong Kong, who everyone thought had been kidnapped, but it turned out had run off to join the anarchists in Spain.

Their lunch came: hot bowls of soup with noodles and dumplings, followed by sweet roasted pork and bowls and bowls of perfect rice. Poppy had never tasted anything like it. A part of her wanted to stay in this café, with these interesting people and this delicious food, forever.

But after the excitement of the day, Poppy suddenly felt tense and exhausted, almost like she was swimming and had swum too long, and might drown.

The woods are mine, she thought. *The orchards are mine. My birch trees, my blue jays, my hawks.*

They finished lunch and got back in the car and drove back to Killington Manor. Poppy sat in the backseat and Aunt Julia and Olivia sat in the front again, still talking about cases and crimes and mysteries. Poppy started to doze off. But then she startled awake and sat up. She realized she had forgotten the most important question.

"Aunt Julia? Olivia?" Poppy said.

"Yes?" Olivia said.

"Did we find out who killed Mrs. Kitty?"

"Not yet," Aunt Julia said. "But we will soon."

It was three o'clock by the time they got home. The adults were in the great hall again, starting early with cocktails and music. Poppy went to her room to take a nap, and Aunt Julia did the same. Olivia had butchering to do, and went to work in the kitchen.

Poppy thought how unfair it was that Olivia had to work while Poppy got to take a nap. When the house was hers, she decided, she would have someone else work, so Olivia could nap, too. After all, they were friends now, or almost. But what about that other person, the one who would replace Olivia? When would *they* nap? What if Poppy became friends with them, too? The whole question was muddy and confusing to Poppy, and she'd had enough new thoughts over the past two days. She kicked off her shoes and got into bed fully dressed, and pulled the blankets over her. She felt like electricity was running through her, but too much of it, wearing her thin, and she fell asleep in minutes.

CHAPTER TEN

An hour later, Poppy woke up to a knock on her door. Her head felt wet and confused, and she remembered it all over again: Mrs. Kitty, Gregor, the exciting day investigating.

"Come in," she said.

It was Aunt Julia, and with her was Olivia. Poppy shook herself awake, got out of bed, realized there was no place else to sit, and sat back down on the bed. Olivia sat next to her, and Aunt Julia stood. Both Olivia and Aunt Julia looked eager and excited, with bright eyes.

"What happened?" Poppy asked.

"We've been investigating," Aunt Julia said.

"What did you find?" Poppy asked.

"Much," Aunt Julia said. "But I'm not sure we ought to discuss it here. Let's go for a walk."

Poppy quickly got her shoes back on, and a light coat, and they went outside together through the servants' quarters, avoiding the other Killingtons. The sun was going down, and a chill was coming in from the ocean as they walked toward the woods.

"Well," Olivia said. "We called Gregor—it was cyanide all right. And I've done a little digging about who was where when Saturday night. Being a hunter, I usually go to bed by nine and wake up with the sun. I didn't know what was going on here after dark—quite a bit, it turns out."

They reached the edge of the woods but, to Poppy's relief, didn't enter. Instead, they kept walking toward the fruit orchard.

"First I started with Charlotte," Olivia went on. "She was sound asleep all night, like every night. Of course I cross-checked all the stories: Everyone backed her up. She's like me—early bed, early rise, no funny business. Next I went out in the woods with my rifle—that's what I do most days, and I didn't want to draw any attention by skipping a day. So I run into Thomas, the groundskeeper, just about here, actually. He was getting some early fruit—Charlotte'll start apple butter tomorrow. We talk a bit about the weather—it took a cold turn this afternoon—and I tell him people are going to be investigating the lady's murder, and he better have his story straight. Tell him I used to be a cop and if he wants I can help him figure it all out. We both know they're going to blame the help, case like this. He hems and haws for a bit, I tell him I'll keep his secrets, he tells me he was with Katherine."

"Katherine?" Poppy asked.

"That's the young maid," Olivia said. "The pretty one. But that's all he says. Says you've got to respect a girl's privacy, and I ought to talk to her. Says he's got his self-respect to put before anything else, even trouble with the cops. So of course that gets me interested, and I go and find Katherine. She's in the laundry room, folding sheets. She tells me—"

Suddenly Olivia stopped and looked at Aunt Julia, a question on her face. Aunt Julia nodded, and Olivia went on.

"She tells me sometimes your uncle Jacob comes—well, he visits her at night sometimes. She doesn't like these visits, not at all."

Poppy frowned. She felt a creeping, crawling feeling inside she couldn't quite make sense of. Her uncle? Going to the maid's room? She corrected herself: *Katherine's* room. Somehow knowing the maid's name made the knowledge more disturbing. A maid was just a maid, but Katherine was a real person, just a few years older than Poppy, with feelings and thoughts just like Poppy had.

"So on Friday," Olivia went on, "Thomas found her crying in the tool shed. She told him what was going on. So the next night—Saturday night—Thomas and Henry, the gardener, sat in her room all night, playing cards on the floor. Around midnight, someone opens the door, surprise surprise, there he is—Jacob. Thomas and Henry—Katherine did a good impression for me, she's a funny girl—act innocent as can be, ask Jacob what he needs, can they help him, *yes sir, no sir*. They say Katherine's their cousin—she ain't—and they like to play cards together. Of course Jacob has nothing to say, makes up some horseshit about seeing a light on. Thomas and Henry heard him go right back to bed after that. And Thomas won five bucks off Henry in gin. So that's four people accounted for. And Miss Daisy, apparently she was in her room crying about it all night, can hardly blame her, but, in any case, that's five."

Poppy felt a little sick from this story. She thought about Katherine, scared and alone in her room, dreading Jacob's visits.

"Next," Olivia said, "I go down to the garage so I can run into Johnny, the driver. Tell him I was following a deer, not true, but we start talking, tell him the same thing: Cops are gonna be asking questions and I don't want to see the help screwed over, so if he tells me where he was I can help him smooth out any rough edges. Johnny tells me he was…that he has a very close friendship with those friends of your parents, Martin and Peter. They—well, when Martin and Peter are here, they all like to get together to talk."

"But what do they talk about?" Poppy asked. "In the middle of the night?"

Poppy noticed that both Aunt Julia and Olivia were holding back smiles. Poppy was confused.

"They have certain interests in common," Aunt Julia said.

"Yeah, that's it," Olivia said. "They all—well, you know, Johnny's the driver and they like talking about cars. So they were up talking about cars most of the night."

"Now," Aunt Julia said, "your father was in his study all night. Katherine said he sleeps there most nights, listening to music and drinking whiskey. Her room is by the stairs, so she would have heard if he'd gone anywhere. And with that, we're very close to an answer."

"So did you crack the case?" Poppy asked.

"I think we have," Aunt Julia said—but Poppy noticed her eyes turned down a bit as she said it, as if she were worried. "And we're going to tell everyone now. But you might want to wait here. And I want you to know— whatever happens tonight, we'll make sure you're taken care of. We won't let you drift away."

Aunt Julia took Poppy's hand in her own, her skin papery and cool. Poppy felt her head spin a little. She missed Mrs. Kitty. She felt something burning inside her—a desire to forget all this, to stick her head under the blankets and forget she'd ever started solving the Mystery at Killington Manor. But even stronger was a desire to know the answer—for Mrs. Kitty, for herself, and for some other reason she couldn't exactly name. Later in life she would learn the word for that feeling: courage.

"I want to be there," Poppy said. "No matter what it is—I'd rather be there than not."

Olivia nodded, and the three of them went back to the house and into the great hall, where the adults had gathered for more cocktails before dinner.

CHAPTER ELEVEN

Olivia and Poppy waited by the doorway to the great hall, while Julia strode right in. All the adults were in there again, with cocktails and music. Before anything else, Aunt Julia fixed herself a whiskey and soda, with very little soda and two maraschino cherries, at the bar. Then she walked to the record player and took the needle off the record and placed it on its cradle.

Everyone in the room turned to look at her.

"If I can have everyone's attention for a moment," Aunt Julia began. "I know us old ladies can have excessive demands. But I believe I've figured something out—who killed Livinia Killington."

Everyone looked at Aunt Julia. Poppy felt a sick tension in her stomach, and her chest and hands felt tight.

"Aunt Julia," Josh said, with gentle irritation. "No one killed Grandmother. She was old, and she passed in her sleep."

"She did not," Aunt Julia said. "She was poisoned by cyanide. A blue tinge on her lips led me to suspect this, and the coroner confirmed it. The only question is, who brought her the cyanide, and when?"

Everyone looked at each other, confused.

"Really," Maisie said. "We know this is hard for you.

Grandmother was your special friend. But—"

Aunt Julia kept talking.

"The *when*, I can establish fairly clearly. I was with her the entire time from when she arrived until she went to bed around midnight. By seven-thirty the next morning, when she'd been found, her body was cool—it was a chilly night, and her fire was out—and stiff. Cyanide kills rapidly, but even in low temperatures, a body takes a few hours to chill. So she was given the poison sometime between, probably, midnight and three-thirty a.m., in a teacup everyone here had access to, by an unknown party. That would be our murderer."

Maisie and Daisy made sounds like *Oh* and *Ugh* and said *Come on now*, but Aunt Julia went on.

"I've asked a few questions," Aunt Julia went on. "Martin and Peter, of course, had no obvious motivation. But motivations for murder can be complicated and surprising."

Peter and Martin both froze. They knew what their alibi was, but they were not keen for that knowledge to spread.

Aunt Julia went on, "But they're well cleared in their alibi." Peter and Martin unfroze. "Jacob, I have to admit, was a prime suspect. But Jacob, too," she said with a sharp look at Jacob, "was otherwise engaged, however dismayingly so."

Daisy, too, shot a sharp look at Jacob. Jacob kept his head high and his chin out, trying to ignore them. But Poppy saw, around his eyes, some combination of shame and arrogance, and she knew that he knew he was in the wrong.

The truth shows itself, Poppy thought. *Truth will come out. Something must win this, and it must be the truth, it must.*

"Josh," Aunt Julia said, "is a passive man, and incapable of murder. But he's been thoroughly cleared nonetheless—he was observed to be in his study all night, having had a few too many whiskeys. And, of course, you will wonder about the staff. I assure you everyone who works here was accounted for on the night of the murder. And as for myself, my only alibi is Liv herself. For clarity's sake, let me be clear I had nothing to gain from killing my oldest friend.

"So now, of course, we turn to Daisy."

Daisy and Maisie both stood up, outraged.

"I won't tolerate this," Maisie said. "You're a guest in this home."

"*Were* a guest," Daisy said. "We'd like you to leave."

"Oh no," Aunt Julia said. Suddenly she sounded different to Poppy than she had before—serious and strong, and somehow, at the same time, heartbroken. "I'm not going anywhere. You can drag me out of here if you like, but you won't. It would be unseemly.

"The world is not a fair place. The deaths of the young and wealthy and beautiful are mourned in public; the deaths of the old, the infirm, the immigrant, and the impoverished are mourned privately, but with no less sorrow. Justice is not brought to these crimes. To those in power, some people are of consequence and some are not. But not when I have a say in it—and I believe, here, I do. With each death, an entire world is extinguished, very often for another person's greed. Vengeance is for God, but justice is for earth, and that's what we must always look toward, and justice will come to this murder if it's the last thing I do—and, at my age, it may well be. Livinia's killer will not sleep in a feather bed and spend Livinia's money on trifles while my dear friend turns to dust, forgotten. That will not be the case, not as long as I have breath in my body."

The adults looked at each other uncomfortably. No one was going to try to drag her out now. Aunt Julia went on, "And so I will continue. Daisy, your sobbing in your room was overheard that night, by many. I'm sorry to tell you your suspicions about your husband were correct. But your alibi holds—no one saw or heard you leave your room all night. You may sit down, Daisy."

And suddenly Poppy knew. She knew, but she didn't want to know.

Poppy fought back tears. And now she wished she had never started looking into the Mystery at Killington Manor. She wanted to jump up and tell Aunt Julia to shut up: A quick image came to Poppy's head of smacking the old woman to make her stop talking, forever.

Then she thought: *I cannot let this go. Mrs. Kitty loved me. Mrs. Kitty knew me. Only her, and no one but her. I must do right by her, her above anyone else.*

Poppy began to shiver, knowing what was coming.

Daisy's face was white. She looked at her sister. Now everyone else looked at Maisie, too.

"Stop it!" Maisie said. She put her hands over her ears, as if not hearing the truth could protect her from it. It had worked for her so far, in her forty-three years, but it would not work now. "Stop talking right now!"

"I will not," Aunt Julia said. "You're the only person who *could* have done it, my dear. You were the only person with no alibi for the time of the murder, and you and your sister had the most to gain from Mrs. Killington's death. You did not know the will had been changed—you did not know how little you had to gain. But perhaps you would have done it anyway. I know you better than you think, Maisie. I've had more than forty years to observe you, and you have not changed. There is one word that has defined your life, and that word is *more*. More money, more men, more clothes, more jewelry and homes and horses and cars. I do take some blame myself. I could have tried harder to steer you to a better path." Aunt Julia glanced at Poppy with her keen sparrow eyes. "This is a mistake I will not make again. Never again will I idly watch a young person become ruined by such stupidity. You killed Livinia Killington, and you will pay."

"This is insane," Maisie said, hands finally back down by her sides. Her regular strength was coming back to her. Poppy could see her mother already molding the truth, shaping the world around her to what she wanted it to be. "Truly mad. You're senile, Aunt Julia. We'll have to make arrangements. You've become demented."

The other adults began to nod. Poppy saw it all slipping away. She wanted to say something, but her mouth was frozen.

"Really," Daisy said. "You'll be much happier, Aunt Julia. They have medicines, and all your meals will be cooked for you."

Josh and Jacob murmured in agreement. Olivia hung back by the doorway. Her face was tight. The tide seemed to be turning, as it always did, toward what Maisie wanted.

I can't, Poppy thought. *I can't do this.* But it applied

equally either way: She couldn't speak, and she couldn't not speak. She couldn't do what was right, and she couldn't do what was wrong. All of it was impossible.

So I must do an impossible thing, she thought, and she spoke.

"But, Momma," Poppy said, looking at the floor, unable to look her mother in the eye. "I heard you."

Everyone looked at Poppy.

Poppy loved her mother very much. She would always love her mother, with more passion than she would ever love anyone else. She loved her mother's smell, gin and musky, floral perfume; her unwillingness to be kind for the sake of kindness (which took a courage Poppy was sure she would never have); the way she turned those same often-unkind words into charm and humor. Poppy loved every item from her mother's vast wardrobe, but especially loved the pieces she wore most often: her Dior dresses, her Chanel suits, the dungarees and Josh's old khaki pants she wore when she toured the grounds or walked in the woods. She loved the crisp way her mother ordered the help—and Poppy—around. She loved her mother most of all when she drank too much and came into Poppy's room at night to tell long, rambling stories about why she'd married the wrong man, how the world was not fair to her, how she should have been a poet, or married a richer man, or run away with someone called Lawrence. Those moments were the closest they would ever be.

Poppy loved her mother. But she didn't like her mother. She knew her mother was a wild animal, just barely tamed. If you petted her just right and offered her treats, in the form of compliments and imitation and obedience, she would purr and smile and let you stay close. But one misstep, and she would lash out, and scratch. All the more so since Poppy had stopped being a child, and had become something closer to an adult. With every step Poppy took toward being a woman, her mother saw something Poppy was doing wrong. Her hair was wrong, her clothes were never right, her interests were shameful. And most shameful of all was Poppy's garden.

Of course they had a formal garden in front of the house, and a few topiary hedges, shaped like elephants, further down the drive. Down the hill, by the woods, was a small fruit orchard with apple and pear trees, which the gardener pruned every other year. At the edge of the orchard was a blackberry bramble where Poppy loved to pick berries in the summer. In between the house and the orchard was the kitchen garden, which Charlotte, the cook, wouldn't let the gardener touch, and this was the garden that fascinated Poppy. It wasn't pretty, but it was beautiful. Rows of mustard greens and broccoli in the winter; strawberries and peas, with their bright flowers and efficient twig frames, in the spring; sweet fragrant tomatoes in August and September; a row of herbs that shifted and died and came back to life all season: thyme, parsley, flowering mint. Charlotte used her herbs for cooking, but also for teas she would make to ward off colds and stomachaches and sleepless nights. The staff all took the teas with no fuss, but the Killingtons lightly mocked Charlotte's herbal teas, calling them *potions* or *witch teas*, unless the doctor wasn't available or couldn't help and then they begrudgingly told her to go make "one of her drinks."

Poppy loved the garden. Charlotte didn't like Poppy much, but in the kitchen garden, in her loveless way, Charlotte would let Poppy follow her around and even sometimes drop little hints for her: Plant seeds when the moon is waxing, but harvest during the wane. Plant the tomatoes by the peas, but far from the mustard. Charlotte even had a log she'd had the groundsman move from the forest where hen-of-the-woods mushrooms grew. Those mushrooms were Poppy's favorite food, in no small part because she'd seen them grow. Charlotte made them in brandy sauce with beef.

A year ago, after much begging and nagging from Poppy, everyone agreed she could have a little garden of her own. She'd never been so excited, ever. First she bought a plain small notebook at the stationery shop in town and sketched the whole thing out, just like she'd seen Charlotte and Henry do. She knew she wanted her own tomatoes for summer, and cabbage for fall, and every herb she could possibly find: chives and lemon balm and mint and sage. Thomas found a little time to help Poppy, who'd never truly had her hands in the dirt before, get it all started. On the border, Poppy planted cuttings Henry grudgingly gave her from his pansies and miniature roses, and Thomas dug up some wild violets for her to replant.

The first few weeks with her garden were the happiest days of Poppy's life. Soon she was ordering books on botany and agriculture and mycology from the bookstore, one book providing the path to the next, and Poppy tore through them all. Her mind spun joyfully with soil composition, fertilizers, ladybugs and aphids, moon phases and words to never say around hydrangeas. Every morning she woke up excited, and could hardly wait to get dressed in her old dungarees and get outside and water and plant and weed and observe.

But then she made a mistake. The biggest mistake. It was over dinner with Maisie and Daisy and Jacob and Josh. There were no guests that night, just the twins and the husbands and Poppy, and the adults were all in rotten moods—Poppy had heard whispers of a late check and a silver set that might have to be sold. But Poppy was so happy and excited about her garden that she failed to adequately read Maisie's mood—and that was the most important thing, always the most important thing. To read Maisie's mood, and know what might be tolerated and what, under any circumstances, would not.

Poppy's mother had always accused her of being "excitable," and now, as Poppy was going on and on about sage and violets and nitrogen, Maisie turned to her with a sharp look and said, "Just when I thought you couldn't get any more tiresome, Pop, you're stealing the gardener's job. Maybe you ought to go eat in the kitchen with the help."

Everyone laughed, and Poppy felt her face turn crimson with shame—shame at her stupid hobby, her utter failure at being a daughter Maisie was proud of, and most of all at the idea that she had more in common with the staff, whose names she still didn't know, than her own family. In the hours and years to come, she would consider that a compliment. But she didn't then.

Maisie quickly turned away from Poppy and crisply changed the subject. Poppy was so sick with herself that she burned inside, and could barely eat. She was sure she even saw the skinny serving girl—Katherine—shoot her a small look of sympathy, which made her feel even lower.

Poppy didn't speak a word through the rest of the dinner.

When the meal was done, Poppy stayed at the table for a long time, so frozen by shame that she was unable to move. Even Charlotte came out and tried to be nice— well, nice for Charlotte. She plunked a piece of her special coconut cake in front of Poppy.

"One slice left," Charlotte said gruffly. "We need the room in the pantry. Might as well eat it."

But Charlotte's pity only made her feel worse.

The sun had gone down. Poppy was so full of horrible feelings that she couldn't stand to be herself. She didn't want to be Poppy anymore, ever again. Overwhelmed, she got up from the table and ran out to her garden. She sobbed with rage as she ripped out the rosemary and the basil and kicked over the mustard and kale. She hated them—they'd made her look stupid and childish. She felt a little better, but not better enough, and so she went to her room and threw all her gardening books on the floor, and then picked them up and threw them all again. She got into bed and thought she would cry herself to sleep.

But as the night wore on, and she couldn't sleep, she stopped crying. Bit by bit, she saw that there was nothing wrong with her garden at all. There were women who were famous for their gardens. And other people had interests and hobbies and all kinds of crafts. Her mother's friend Beatrice embroidered pillowcases. Once Poppy had stayed with her friend Midge for the weekend and Midge's mother spent the whole weekend painting a picture of a boat, and no one called her names or laughed at her—instead, at the end of the weekend the whole family came to look at it, and everyone acted like it was something special, something good. Like it was just another reason to love her.

The problem wasn't Poppy or her garden. It was Maisie. And that was when Poppy knew: that she loved her mother, but didn't like her, and she vowed to never let her mother into her heart again. No more fighting for Maisie's attention, no more trying to please Maisie with perfume and high-heeled shoes, no more excitement over those rare moments when Maisie would toss Poppy a kind word or give her a hug or kiss or, after a few drinks, sit next to Poppy and tell her her secrets. In the weeks to come, the whole world changed for Poppy as she methodically cut her mother off from her affection. But nothing seemed to change for Maisie, or anyone else. No one else seemed to notice any change at all. That was when Poppy realized she didn't really exist in Killington Manor—not to anyone but Mrs. Kitty. To Maisie and Daisy and Josh and Jacob, Poppy was as important as a new cocktail ring or record player, and just as disposable. Only to Mrs. Kitty was she real.

Then Poppy felt terrible for another reason—she'd ruined her garden and trashed her gardening books. Like her mother, she'd been cruel to the exact things that had shown her so much love. She straightened up all her books and rearranged her bookshelf to give her gardening books the place of pride, right on the top shelf. Then she made a careful list of new books she would buy tomorrow. She didn't sleep at all, and as soon as the sun came up, she got dressed in her dungarees and an old shirt and went back out to her garden.

Poppy's little patch was not far from the kitchen garden, and as the morning came she saw Charlotte standing with Thomas, looking over Poppy's little plot. She felt sick inside, wondering if they knew how mortifyingly cruel her own mother had been to her, and how childish she'd been in response. She wanted to turn back, but she stopped herself. *No one will ruin this for me*, she thought, *not ever again.*

But to Poppy's surprise, when she reached them, Charlotte and Thomas were just as they always were—Charlotte grumpy and silent and Thomas calm and friendly.

"Looks like a fox got in," Thomas said. "Come on, we'll clean it up together. And how about we build a taller fence to keep it safe?"

Poppy smiled for the first time since she'd stopped speaking at dinner the night before. She felt so happy and thankful she thought she might cry all over again, but she held it back. She was almost sure that he knew how stupid she'd been, and almost sure that he forgave her. All morning, she kept expecting Thomas to give her a talk, or explain to her what she'd done wrong, or make sure she knew this was her last chance, the very last one, because she was too much trouble and too much worry and too much, or not enough, of everything.

But that didn't happen. If Thomas thought Poppy was too much or too little, he kept it to himself, and went about his work with quiet industriousness as always, occasionally pointing out to her how the rosemary could be slightly better placed to catch the sun or how some broccoli might be worth trying before it got too late. Thomas helped her fix what she'd destroyed—nearly everything, to Poppy's tremendous relief, could be saved—and then they went into the woods and found good twigs and spent the rest of the morning building a fence. And she didn't like her mother anymore.

Maisie never mentioned the garden again.

This made it easier for Poppy to say what she needed to say now, in the great hall.

"I heard you," Poppy said again to her mother. "You

weren't asleep all night. I heard you walking in the hallway."

Her mother didn't even look at her. But everyone else did.

"Nonsense," Maisie said. "You're always making up stories."

"I never make up stories," Poppy said. "You never let me. You called my stories stupid and unimaginative. You killed Mrs. Kitty and you did it for the worst reason—for money. You never loved her at all. You always wanted her money, and now you're never going to get it, because everyone will know."

Maisie turned and glared at her.

"Go to your room right now," Maisie said. "Leave the adults be."

But Poppy didn't move, and while she and Maisie glared at each other, someone knocked on the door. Maisie tore her gaze from her daughter and walked to the front door to answer it.

"That might be the police," Aunt Julia said. "I asked them to drop by."

The police officer was a man of thirty or forty, clean-shaven and with a fakely sad look on his face. Martin and Peter took his entrance as an opportunity to leave, for the obvious reasons, Poppy guessed to some other country house. The rest of the adults milled around anxiously—especially, of course, Maisie, who was drinking a strong cocktail and smoking one cigarette after another.

Poppy stood up and walked over to Olivia, still standing in the doorway. Maisie glared at her as she walked. *I don't love you*, Poppy thought. *I loved you, and you killed that part of me, and now there's nothing left that loves you anymore.*

"Do you know him?" Poppy asked Olivia, looking at the police officer.

"Yes," Olivia said.

"Is he a good one?" Poppy asked.

"No," Olivia said. Poppy turned and looked at Olivia. Olivia's face was tight and angry.

"Officer Camden," the officer said, introducing himself. "I understand someone thinks there's been a murder?"

Aunt Julia told him the whole story, quickly and elegantly. Officer Camden took notes in a small paperbound notebook.

"And she was how old?" Officer Camden said at the end.

Aunt Julia forced a smile and opened her mouth to answer, but Maisie interrupted.

"You must forgive our guest," Maisie said, all steel behind a knowing smile. "The deceased was a dear friend, and she's not herself."

"Tragedy does strike," Officer Camden said.

"The tragedy was murder," Aunt Julia said.

"The tragedy," Maisie said, "was a woman's life ending at her natural time."

"We have evidence," Aunt Julia said. "She was poisoned. And if you search this house and the dumping grounds, I'm confident you'll find an empty bottle of cyanide."

"Ridiculous," Maisie said. "Aunt Julia, I must insist you let this inane line of reasoning go. You've let your imagination run wild."

Poppy recognized the sweet, clever voice her mother used now. Poppy had heard her use it before, when Maisie wanted to persuade and convince. *And lie,* Poppy thought now. *She lies and lies and no one stops her. But I will. She could have loved me. Every single day, she could have loved me, and did not.*

Maisie put a hand on Officer Camden's arm. "We may get further if we can discuss this privately." She glared at Aunt Julia with an exaggerated look. "Shall we step into the study?"

"That might be for the best," Officer Camden said. Daisy joined her sister, and Maisie, Daisy, and the officer went into the study and closed the door behind them.

No one talked. Aunt Julia came over to stand by Olivia and Poppy.

"What are they doing?" Poppy whispered to Olivia.

Olivia didn't say anything, just shook her head and looked strangely sad. So did Aunt Julia. Neither of them said anything.

They waited for five or ten minutes. Poppy was sure that any moment, the police officer would emerge from the study with Maisie in handcuffs, ready to take her away for murdering Mrs. Kitty.

But that didn't happen. Instead, they all walked out together—Daisy and Maisie and Officer Camden— smiling. No one was holding on to anyone. No one was in handcuffs.

Daisy and Maisie walked the police officer to the door. Maisie said, "We're so pleased to be able to help. The station could use some sprucing up."

"We appreciate it," the officer said. "The donation will be very useful. A happy ending for all."

Poppy saw Olivia's face grow stern. She felt her own face grow hot. She knew she should stay quiet, but she couldn't. Instead, she called out, "It wasn't a happy ending for Mrs. Kitty!"

Her mother turned and glared at her. But Maisie quickly remembered to paint her smile back on. The officer caught sight of Olivia on the staircase. They looked at each other and said nothing and then the officer looked away.

"Don't worry," Aunt Julia said to Poppy, quietly. "Let them be. There's always another way."

The policeman left. The twins and the husbands breathed sighs of relief.

"Well, that's all done," Maisie said. She looked exhausted. "Fortunately, Aunt Julia, the police are not prone to believe senile women. You will please leave this house tonight."

"I will," Aunt Julia said, dumb and sweet again, like she'd been in the bank. "Right after dinner. I can't apologize enough, Maisie. Perhaps you're right. My age may be catching up with me."

Daisy and Maisie and the husbands, all looking like they'd made it through a shipwreck—disturbed and worn through, but thankful—headed to the stairs to freshen up after their trials.

At the foot of the staircase, Maisie paused and turned toward Poppy. She frowned.

"Go on," she said sharply. "Go dress for dinner. Your mother's had a hard day. We have rules in this house."

Poppy now felt, for the first time in her life, cold inside, like ice. Usually she was overtaken with some burning emotion or other, carried away by her feelings before she even knew what those feelings were. But now she felt nothing—at least nothing she could name. Just cold and hard.

"In a moment, Mother," Poppy said.

Maisie nodded, managing to fill the nod with disapproval, and turned and climbed up the stairs.

"I know a few decent guys in Boston," Olivia said. But her tone didn't hold much hope.

"If they can be trusted," Aunt Julia said.

"And if we can get them to come out here," Olivia said.

"Come on," Poppy said. "We all have to get ready for dinner."

Olivia wrinkled her brow. Aunt Julia looked at Poppy with a question on her face. Poppy knew she had to earn her place with them, and she wasn't earning it now. *They think they were wrong about me*, Poppy thought. *They will see. They will see.*

A plan began to form in Poppy's head.

Olivia went back to the kitchen. Aunt Julia went to her room to dress. And Poppy began her plan. But first, Poppy packed up her favorite books in a wooden box and hid them in the woods, under the oldest maple tree, the one they'd tap first in the spring. With the books, she put the ceramic cat that had been Mrs. Kitty's. If her plan didn't work, she was prepared. Then she went back to her room and dressed for dinner, in a white dress and white high heels—no sense in causing a fight now.

Then she went to the garage, and got to work.

CHAPTER TWELVE

Dinner was served late at Killington Manor, for the obvious reasons. The twins, the husbands, Poppy, and Aunt Julia sat around the table. Charlotte had made hen in juniper berries and ladyfinger trifles for dessert. But just before they started to eat, Poppy stood up.

"I'd like…" she said. She was trying for a big voice, a voice with authority, but it came out as a little mumble, so she started again.

"I'd like everyone to come outside. I have a surprise."

This time she managed a voice that sounded as cold as she felt inside. Maisie and Daisy looked at Poppy as if she'd lost her mind. But Aunt Julia stood right up and smiled at her.

"I love surprises," Aunt Julia said, doing a good performance of senility. "Where shall we go?"

"Just outside," Poppy said. "I'll be right out, but you must all go out first. So I can prepare the surprise."

Daisy and Maisie stayed in their chairs. But they saw Aunt Julia heading toward the door, and then the husbands, and begrudgingly followed. Guests gone, Poppy ran into the kitchen and found Olivia.

"I have a plan," Poppy said to Olivia. "But you must get all the staff out to the garden, right now, or it won't work. They could even get hurt."

Olivia looked at her sideways. Poppy could see that she had risen in Olivia's esteem over the course of the day. Olivia had slowly and carefully let Poppy prove herself, and had let Poppy into her world, one hard-earned inch at a time. Now that door was closing all over again. Poppy could see herself turning into Maisie—or worse, Daisy—in Olivia's eyes.

"You have to trust me," Poppy said. "I know I haven't given you reason to. But you have to trust me now."

"OK," Olivia finally said. "I'll get them out."

Poppy could see that Olivia had lost faith in her, even as she did as Poppy asked.

She will see, Poppy thought. *She will see that I'm not like them at all.*

CHAPTER THIRTEEN

Everyone gathered outside, the staff with quiet frustration, the residents with open derision. It was dark, with squares of light from the kitchen windows illuminating the spot where they all stood, in between the kitchen garden and the house, about twenty feet from each. Maisie and Daisy wrapped their arms around themselves to stay warm, while Jacob and Josh shuffled their feet, generating heat.

Poppy, carrying a large watering can, came out to meet them.

"Thank you all for coming," she said. "As you may know, Killington Manor and everything in it was left to me by Mrs.—by my great-grandmother. I have a few years before I come into it all, but in the meantime, I've made a decision."

She looked at her family for what she hoped was the last time.

"I'd like you to leave my house," Poppy said.

Maisie and Daisy laughed. Jacob and Josh scowled. Aunt Julia opened her eyes wide, and then smiled.

Olivia kept her face still and uncommitted. *You will see*, Poppy thought. *I will burn this world to the ground before I become like them.*

"We will do no such thing," Maisie said. "When you come into the estate, *if* you come into the estate, such decisions will be made then. You know, my grandmother was not in her right mind. Not in her right mind at all. We'll see what the lawyers say."

"Well, I have my own lawyer," Poppy said, which drew raised eyebrows from the adults. "And the man at the bank said that everything will be mine. So you can leave now. Or…"

Poppy walked back to the house, and started pouring the contents of the watering can on the wooden walls, splashing liquid all over the trim and the baseboards.

The other Killingtons looked at each other with confusion.

"Poppy," Maisie began, "I'm not sure what point you're trying to prove, but—"

But Maisie stopped when she smelled what was coming out of the watering can.

It wasn't water.

It was gasoline.

Soon everyone else noticed, too.

Poppy pulled a large box of matches out of her pocket.

"Turn around," she said to everyone.

Everyone turned around.

"You will see," Poppy went on, "that the garage is on fire."

Everyone kept looking. As Poppy promised, in a moment they all saw flames coming from the windows in the garage, orange and red against the dark night sky.

Murmurs and shrieks came from her family.

Daisy looked at the servants. "Put it out!" she said.

But the servants didn't move. Instead, they all looked at Poppy. *They don't hate me*, Poppy thought, and it was as if the sun rose inside of her. *They will forgive me, and let me prove myself.*

Poppy looked at Olivia. Now Oliva smiled at her, and Poppy's heart swelled.

"I have raised," Maisie said, "a monster."

"No," Poppy said. "I have been raised by a murderer. You have what you wanted from Mrs. Kitty—money— and I will give you more, so I can be sure you never bother me again. Your cars are at the end of the drive. I had the driver—I mean I *asked* the driver, I mean I asked *Johnny*—to drive them there before I started the fire. You will leave this house tonight, all of you, and turn control of my estate over to Aunt Julia and my lawyer. You can come back another day for your things. Or—"

She took out a match from the box and held it up.

"I will burn Killington Manor down, and you will lose everything."

Aunt Julia let out a sound that was between a laugh and a hoot.

"I'm calling the police," Daisy said.

"It won't matter," Poppy said. "By the time they put out the fire, everything will be gone. All of your dresses and jewelry and records will be ash. All you'll have is what Mrs. Kitty left you. I'll never give you a penny more. And I will fight you in court and all your friends will see who you are. You will leave now with something, or you will leave later with much less."

The garage crackled and boomed as the fire spread across the walls and to the roof.

Poppy struck the match against the side of the box. It lit with a soft crackling sound.

"Leave my house," Poppy said. "Now."

"I think," Aunt Julia said, "she intends to do as she says."

Maisie turned to Aunt Julia. "This is your doing," she said. "You've poisoned my daughter against me."

"No," Aunt Julia said. "You've poisoned this family all by yourself. And your daughter has taken it upon herself to find a cure."

Daisy was the first to turn and walk away, with the cowardice and obedience that had defined her life, head down, ashamed of everything. Following her was Jacob, perhaps hoping to win her back, then Josh, who, in fairness, had never known his daughter at all.

The last to leave was Maisie. She stood and stared at her daughter for a long moment.

"You will regret treating your mother this way," Maisie said. "Nothing good will come of this. It isn't natural."

"I regret," Poppy said, "not having treated you this way for all of my sixteen years. You could have loved me, and I wish you had. But you decided not to."

Finally, Maisie turned and walked to her car, slowly, with great precision, cocktail in hand and her head high.

There was one Killington left at Killington Manor. And all of it was hers.

CHAPTER FOURTEEN

As soon as the other Killingtons were gone, Charlotte, Olivia, Aunt Julia, Poppy, Henry, Thomas, Johnny, and Katherine rushed to put out the fire at the garage. The structure was lost, but they stopped the flames from spreading. Then they carefully washed the gasoline off the house itself and hosed it down with water.

Aunt Julia said that since Charlotte had prepared such a lovely meal, they all ought to eat it. So they all ate together in the kitchen. Henry asked if he could have a drink, and Poppy said, "Of course. Everything here is ours."

I will grow flowers in every room, Poppy thought. *I will grow lemons in the great hall.*

So Henry poured glasses of the best whiskey in the house for everyone, including Poppy, and she drank it in a few big gulps. The ice inside her started to melt, and she felt warm again. After dinner, Olivia started a fire in the fireplace, and Katherine put on a record. Aunt Julia danced with Henry, and Poppy danced with Katherine, and everyone was laughing and talking, and Poppy thought, *This is the most fun anyone has had in this house since Mrs. Kitty lived here.* She realized that with her mother gone, she could cry if she wanted to. But she didn't feel like crying now. The thing that always seemed so elusive to her—happiness—was now all around her. Even if she wasn't entirely ready to jump into it herself, at least she could watch it, hear it, smell it. She would have to learn, she saw, how to enter this strange land.

Poppy learned that Charlotte was a widow and a grandmother and never liked Poppy, or any of the Killingtons, or anyone else she'd cooked for. She said she didn't like most people, and liked the rich the least. Poppy learned that Thomas played chess and read as much as she did, and with great excitement Poppy showed him all her gardening books. Henry had two daughters just about her age who lived in town, and maybe she could meet them someday. Aunt Julia had met the Princess of Siam and flown on twelve airplanes. She learned that Katherine was a little bit in love with Johnny, the chauffeur. And Johnny and Aunt Julia sat in the corner for hours and talked about the war, and shooed Poppy away when she got close.

Late into the night Olivia and Poppy sat by the fireplace.

"Are you from England?" Poppy asked.

"No," Olivia said. "My mom and dad were born in Jamaica, moved to London, then back to Jamaica, then Boston."

"Do you want to be a police officer again?" Poppy asked Olivia.

"On the force?" Olivia said. "No, I wouldn't want to do that again. But doing what we did here? Yeah, I enjoyed that."

They looked at the fire.

"You know," Olivia went on, "when I came to Killington Manor, I thought you were just about the most spoiled thing I ever saw. When I was your age I could cook a meal, fix what was broken, squeeze a dollar out of a dime, and shoot a rabbit at twenty yards. But turns out you have quite a spine, little Poppy."

Poppy's heart swelled. She thought, *My spine will hold me up, and I will never be scared again. My spine has saved me.*

At the end of the night, most of Poppy's guests, who just the day before had been her staff, had fallen asleep on Maisie's bright sofas. Poppy left the house and walked out to her garden. The sun was coming up, and the sky was pink-gray. She saw some weeds growing in the lemon verbena and got down on her knees to pull them. She was still in the dress she'd put on for dinner, and Poppy felt the cold wet earth sink through the fabric to her skin, staining the dress. She lay down on the dirt, and felt Mrs. Kitty's warm arm around her. *My rough-and-tumble girl.*

She realized she could work in her garden all day, and no one would tell her to stop, and that was exactly what she would do.

So this is what happiness feels like, thought Poppy, as she felt its golden rays for the first time. She felt lighter than she had ever felt before, as if she could float away, but at the same time as heavy as the dirt she lay on, and as much a part of the earth. *So this is happiness: like seeing clear blue sky after being lost in the woods.*

She rolled in the dirt, ruining her dress, and smiled.

THE END

TEN-SECOND MYSTERY: HOW YOU NEVER SEEM TO GET EXACTLY WHAT YOU WANT, BUT SOMEHOW TIME MOVES MONSTROUSLY FORWARD ANYWAY

I hate it here. Why did it have to be this way?

SOLUTION

I don't know. No one knows. I'm sorry it has to be like this, but here it is. Here we are. You are in the future; I am writing these words in the past; and yet, I care about you, although I may not like you. Why else would I write this? I want to be your friend. Go outside (if you can);

look around with new eyes. This is a new moment and if you wish, you can try to be a new person. But how you are now is just fine with me. It might not be fine for the people who have to live with you and try to love you, though. Wise people tell us that our only chance for happiness is to accept life as it is, not pine for life as we want it to be. Maybe I'll try that today. Sounds hard.

All I can tell you is: If you are reading this, you're alive, and if you're alive, there's hope. And I, probably long gone, would like to hold your hand and whisper in your ear: *Happiness is closer than you think*. And when that happiness recedes, along with sense and logic and meaning, I would like to stand on the beach with you at night and watch the dark ocean come and go and say: *Sometimes I think I have everything, and I think I'm the luckiest girl in the world, and then sometimes I think God forgot about me, and I don't know what I'm going to do. All I have is you, a person in the future I've never met and can't know. Most of my life is lived for you, a beloved stranger, because I want to stand on this beach with you. And if we wait, I think happiness will come back, and maybe this time we can trick it into staying for a while longer, and when it leaves again, at least we will have each other.*

THE END

With gratitude to Donald J. Sobol, R. A. Montgomery,
and the many writers known as Carolyn Keene.

SARA GRAN is the publisher of Dreamland Books and the author of seven previous novels, including *Come Closer* and the Claire DeWitt series.

www.ingramcontent.com/pod-product-compliance
Lightning Source LLC
Chambersburg PA
CBHW071413300726
48976CB00006B/2081